# JEFFREY MARCUS OSHINS

# THE GRAY ANARCHIST

Deep Six Publishers

Deep Six Publishers
Johnson & Associates
406 Santa Fe Place, #3
Santa Barbara, CA 93109
805-683-1200

The Gray Anarchist is a work of fiction. Names, characters, businesses, places, events and incidents are either the product of the author's imagination or used in a fictitious manner. Any resemblance to actual persons, living or dead, or actual events is purely coincidental.

Printed in the United States of America.

Library of Congress Control Number: 2023917754
Publisher's Cataloguing-in-Publication Data
Oshins, Jeffrey Marcus, 1950-

ISBN: 9798987788745 Paperback
ISBN: 9798987788738 Hardback
ISBN: 9798987788769 epub

Summary: Lauren Bastini, a 73-year-old white female environmental activist, wages a terrorist campaign on the United States, leading to a nuclear attack on Washington, D.C. FBI agent George Blum's last assignment is to disrupt the campaign of Senator Allan Hansen. Blum pressures Bastini to say that Hanson was an active member of a radical environmental group when he was a student at the University of California, Berkeley. Hansen's campaign manager, Deirdre Owens, with a taste for erotic bondage, must find a way to fight campaign interference by an overreaching White House and keep her candidate from quitting the race. Bastini vows revenge on Hansen for testifying against the group in college. She kidnaps Hansen and Owens, leading to a wild ride through an Air Force bombing range on the U.S.-Mexico border.

1. Jeffrey Marcus Oshins (author)–Fiction. 2. Politics–Fiction. 3. Washington, D.C.–Fiction. 4. Domestic Terrorism–Fiction. 5. West Virginia.–Fiction. 6. FBI campaign interference–Fiction. 7. U.S. Senate–Fiction. 8. LNG–Fiction. 9 Nuclear power. 10. California political campaign–Fiction. 11. California–Fiction. 12.Political Thriller-Fiction 13. Barry M. Goldwater Air Force Range-Fiction. 14. Arizona – Fiction. 15. U.S. Judiciary-Fiction. 16. FBI COINTELPRO-Fiction. 17. Office of the Director of National Intelligence (ONDI)-Fiction. 18. Los Angeles Police Department. (LAPD)-Fiction. 19. Conservative talk radio-Fiction.

She was more dangerous and more destructive than any foreign terrorist. She was a pair of scissors cutting through the fabric of trust that held a civil community together, allowing democracy to exist. She epitomized the essential threat of terrorism–that a terrorist could be anyone–a grandmother or a white American eco-terrorist from West Virginia–that a single person could attack, destroy, and move about freely in a free society. The terrible truth of modern terrorism is that anyone and everyone could be the enemy. And when everyone is the enemy, there can be no trust, and without trust, there can be no freedom, and without freedom, there can be no democracy.

<hr />

# ACRONYMS

**AD:** Assistant director

**AG:** US Attorney General

**AR-15:** Automatic rifle

**ATF:** US Department of Alcohol, Tobacco, Firearms, and Explosives

**BDSM:** Bondage, discipline, dominance, submission erotic role-playing

**CARONA:** US reconnaissance satellite

**CES Referral:** Counterintelligence and Export Control Section National Security Division, Department of Justice

**CIA:** Central Intelligence Agency

**CL:** Chlorine

**COINTELPRO:** FBI counterintelligence program

**COPCOM:** Law enforcement evidence and intelligence sharing system

**DC:** District of Columbia (Washington)

**DHS:** Department of Homeland Security

**DIA:** Defense Intelligence Agency

**DNI:** Director National Intelligence

**DOE:** US Department of Energy

**DSA:** Domestic Security Association

**FBI:** Federal Bureau of Investigations

**FISA:** Foreign Intelligence Surveillance Act of 1978

**FEMA:** Federal Emergency Management Association

**GPS:** Global positioning system

**HIS:** High-interest suspects

**HSAS:** Department of Homeland Security Terrorism Advisory Level (NTAS)

**HMS:** Her Majesty's Ship

**ID:** Identification

**IED:** Improvised explosive device

**IDIQ:** Government indefinite delivery indefinite quantity contract

**JTTF:** Joint Terrorism Task Force

**LED:** Light

**LNG:** Liquified Natural Gas

**LA:** Los Angeles

**LAPD:** Los Angeles Police Department

**LAX:** Los Angeles Airport

**M-16:** Military automatic rifle

**MAC 10 (MAC):** Semi-automatic Rhodesian firearm

**MAPAD:** Man-portable air defense system

**MLK:** Martin Luther King

**MSNBC:** Left-leaning television news program

**MTD:** Metropolitan Transportation District

**MWEOC:** Mount Weather Emergency Operations Center

**NCTC:** National Counterterrorism Center

**NPP:** Nuclear power plant

**NPR:** National Public Radio

**NSA:** National Security Agency

**ODNI:** Office of the Director of National Intelligence

**NERT:** National Emergency Response Team

**PA:** Public address system or production assistant

**PCH:** Route One Pacific Coast Highway

**RF detector:** Radio frequency detector

**RG-5:** LNG refrigeration tank

**ROTC:** Reserve Officer Training Corp

**RPG-7:** Rifle-propelled grenade launcher

**SEAL team:** US Navy Sea, Air, and Land commando unit

**SUV:** Sports utility vehicle

**USAF:** United States Air Force

**US:** United States

*Cast of Characters is on page 205*

# ONE

## GEORGE BLUM

George Blum didn't take the seat that hadn't been offered. His 235 pounds rested squarely on polished dress shoes. His FBI identification badge hung in the V of a dark suit jacket atop a crisp white shirt that billowed over a ponderous gut. Neatly combed silver hair crowned the stern gaze of a seasoned investigator who'd seen it all.

Before him, Assistant US Attorney Dennis Dalleck spoke into a telephone receiver with the confidence of a con.

"Hansen is a terrorist. He was a terrorist in college. He's a terrorist now."

Impossible not to eavesdrop on the conversation, Blum tried to at least give the appearance of not listening by looking at a plaque on the wall, a dark silhouette of Alexander Hamilton with the words, centered in bold script, *Liberty University College of Law Federalist Society*.

Located in Virginia, the evangelical Christian university sent more students to the present White House on work-study than Princeton. The Federalist Society touted its particular attention to the intent of the founding fathers. Blum thought Dalleck must have missed the lecture about not using the power of the state against political opponents.

Blum's law classes had been at night. Five years of missed bedtime stories with his young kids to get ahead in the bureau.

Dalleck's words were a melodious betrayal of the memorandum that

Justice Department employees "may never select the timing of investigative steps or criminal charges for the purpose of affecting any election, or for the purpose of giving an advantage or disadvantage to any candidate or political party."

"Won't be election interference if we do it right. We'll get Hansen. Even California isn't going to elect an acknowledged terrorist. I got my man here working on it."

Dalleck ended his call and studied Blum across the smooth surface of a desk clear of the files and legal forms Blum was used to seeing in a judiciary office.

"You know they started it. They weaponized Justice," Dalleck said as if to reassure Blum that it was all right to use the FBI to defeat a political opponent.

The country was evenly divided into two camps. Blum had seen the cycles–the arrogant left, the righteous right.

On the right, Dalleck's side had the White House, the Supreme Court, and the House of Representatives. Allan Hansen stood in their way of full control of the Senate and the whole US government.

Faith in impartial and equal justice was crumbling under the grinding tread of *us* and *them*. When all you heard were your views echoed back at you–*us* against *them*–and every means justifies the end, it became hard to identify real threats.

Not that Blum minded helping to defeat the leading opponent of the Sentinel Act, which would grant the bureau more tools to collect electronic evidence about US citizens. But running a counterintelligence operation against a sitting US senator was touchy business. Blum had to keep the bureau's fingerprints off the operation.

Dalleck ran his tongue over a thick lower lip. "The White House is disappointed in the way this procedure is going," he said as if critiquing a gall bladder operation.

Blum got the message that this was not a rogue operation but was directed from the top.

The FBI had preserved its own culture and standards until this president accused the bureau of spying on his campaign and not going after his enemies. Now a sizable portion of the public on both sides had lost trust in the FBI.

Maybe his bosses assigned him this dirty work to appease the president. Or maybe to make sure the FBI wasn't identified as interfering in Allan Hansen's campaign. Either way, it was dicey.

Blum's caution was built on three decades of operations that had gone wrong. And what could possibly go wrong with the FBI sabotaging the campaign of a United States senator?

Blum rule number 1: *The law of unintended consequences lurks inside an operation.* Push on one side of the balloon, and the other side expands. Send in a giraffe, and out comes a tiger. Stings, broken doors, screaming women, crying men–he'd learned to slow down when the crazy meters jumped to red, and this was bouncing far right.

"You testified against the Oakland Four. How come Hansen wasn't identified as the fourth conspirator?" Dalleck asked.

"He was given immunity for testifying against Jacob Gillium and Lauren Bastini," Blum explained.

Dalleck rocked forward in his ergonomic office chair. "Berkeley! How could California have a senator from Berkeley? Hansen was part of the gang. Why don't we have a record of his arrest?"

"Sealed and destroyed when he cooperated with the government."

"But you don't know for sure that the records were destroyed?"

*And I don't know your father wasn't a goat.*

Dalleck waved his forefinger around in a froth. "Keep looking. Maybe somebody took them home with them. Find them." Dalleck tapped the back of his finger against his overbite and narrowed his eyes in concentration. "Where's Lauren Bastini?" he asked.

"West Virginia. She makes honey."

"Honey? What is she, a goddamn bee? Put more pressure on her!" Dalleck demanded. "Send some boys up to have a little talk with Ms. Bastini. Convince her to help us defeat this liberal cocksucker."

He said *liberal* like the red hunters used to say *Commie*. The president had lost restraint and called his opponents Communists.

A career in the era of limits raised more Blum rules:

Blum rule number 2: *Beware of true believers–those who would die for their cause.*

The will to survive was the reason relative peace existed in a nation armed, alienated, and ready to shoot.

Blum rule number 3: *Do not activate a dormant threat.* Bastini might be seventy-three years old, but she could and would go hot if mishandled.

"What kind of pressure?"

Dalleck's eyebrows arched over his golf course-tanned cheeks as if Blum had made a joke.

"What the hell do you think your assignment is? Go out there and tell Jacob Gillium and Lauren Bastini we're going to put their asses back in jail unless they publicly say what we all know. Allan Hansen is a goddamn bomb-throwing Berkeley radical."

For a moment, Blum focused on the federal government's prosecuting attorney, who didn't seem to know or care that FBI worked for all the American people, not for him and the minority of voters who'd put him in power.

Dalleck's voice rose, and he pounded his fist on the desk. "I mean, Jesus! Blum! We must defeat Allan Hansen. He's a danger to the nation. The lives of thousands, millions of Americans depend on us defeating him. Now, I want you to go back out there and squeeze these terrorists' nuts until they say what we all know. That Allan Hansen was and is a terrorist."

———◆———

Blum's wife, Franny, liked it when he took her on jobs. He'd gone crazy for her, as had a few other agents when she'd booked evidence at the bureau many years and three grown kids ago.

They avoided the valet parking service at the movie star's oceanfront home and parked a quarter mile down the Pacific Coast Highway in a restaurant lot.

Franny, dressed in five-pocket jeans and an Apolline cropped jacket, plump, if not fat, barely came up to his shoulder, but Blum had to hustle to keep up with her as they walked beside the busy highway cut between steep hillsides and cheek-by-jowl beachside homes.

They passed through an open gate and walked up a driveway lined with towering palms and flower beds. They were purposely one of the first to arrive. Still, six people were ahead of them in a security line. Blum overheard a woman in the line say that she just wanted to see if she looked as much like Barbara Stein as people said she did. Blum thought the heavily touched-up woman vaguely resembled the actress when she'd portrayed a good-hearted Las Vegas hooker. A gay couple behind them, hyped up like they were on amphetamines, kept jabbering about "Bababwa."

Blum didn't see Jake Gillium. He'd sent Gillium one of the thousand-dollar tickets to the fundraiser with a handwritten note: *The senator would like to see you.*

Highly unlikely that either Hansen or Gillium would recognize him. If they did, that would be more pressure to cooperate.

Thirty-five years ago, rail-thin, long-haired, calling himself Cliffy, Blum's first assignment in the FBI Counterintelligence Program–COINTELPRO–had been to infiltrate an eco-terrorist group in Berkeley. A misguided bunch of yahoos the press called the Oakland Four thought they were defending the environment with crimes against businesses. Blum had tipped law enforcement that Lauren Bastini and Jimmy Tolver were going to firebomb the Monsanto Company's biotech research facility in Berkeley.

In a shootout with the police, the bomb had ignited, killing Tolver and burning the skin off Bastini. Blum regretted the death and injury, but the operation had sent a powerful message to other eco-terrorists that the bureau meant business.

He had collected evidence that Allan Hansen, then a freshman at Cal, had been a coconspirator. Hansen had avoided prosecution by testifying against his roommate, Jake Gillium.

Now, not a far reach those thirty-five years later, Gillium would want revenge against Hansen by confirming he'd been an active member of the terrorist gang. The object of this operation was to get pictures and, if possible, audio of the two together. They might even discuss Hansen's past involvement in the Oakland Four.

"No cameras or cellphones," announced a Latino man with *SECURITY* printed on a blue windbreaker.

The Blums presented their tickets and provided fake names and email addresses. Blum left a burner phone with a coat check girl and entered a separate line for men. A security wand did not detect a camera disguised as black reading glasses or the brown prescription bottle holding translucent-strip microphones, each with enough power to reach the recorder in the trunk of his car.

In a foyer, Hansen campaign workers sat behind a table greeting guests and giving them name tags. Large windows in the living room blended indoors and out with sweeping ocean views.

They stepped outside into the backyard, where a buffet table and bar were set up beside a large infinity pool. Beyond a seawall of large boulders, the late-afternoon sun reflected off calm blue water that rolled in low, foam-capped waves up a narrow stretch of sand.

A quick swipe of Blum's hand on the sandstone sculpture of a seagull attached the first microphone that hardly appeared as a smudge.

A waitress offered them canapés from a silver tray.

"Hey, you look like you're coming undone back there," Blum said. He placed another microphone as he tightened the bow of her apron.

"Thanks," she said with a curious expression as if he was trying to cop a feel, evidently excusing him because of his age and Franny smiling at his side.

A bustling woman was preparing silver trays of canapés in a makeshift kitchen inside an open tent. "May I help you, sir?" she asked as he ran his hand over the side of a tray of bruschetta.

"Oh, I was wondering if you had a business card."

She smiled. "I'm busy, as you can see. Can't talk now, but after things settle down, I'd be happy to give you a brochure."

"Sorry. I shouldn't be bothering you. I'll look for you later."

He put a microphone on a vase of flowers on a white-tablecloth-covered table where a bar had been set and another on a woven cloth atop a black piano in the living room.

The place was wired now. The camera in his glasses could be activated with a touch of a thin button in his pocket, but it wouldn't make a difference if Gillium didn't rise to the bait.

In the meantime, he and Franny enjoyed being in the home of a Hollywood star.

# TWO

## DEIRDRE OWENS

Deirdre Owens exuded an air of professional elegance as she surveyed the setup at the Stein fundraiser. A classic pin-striped skirt suit evidenced a polished demeanor and athletic physique. A white blouse with a wing collar added a touch of sophistication to an outfit that allowed her to adapt her style to different situations as the campaign manager of a statewide California Senate campaign.

Having trained in martial arts and maintained a disciplined diet, Deirdre had sculpted her body into a lean and muscular figure. At forty-one years old, a long, slender face pulled forward at the bottom by a strong jaw gave her a distinctive look. Her lips were wide and full, subtly hinting at a smirk rather than a smile conveying a sense of shrewdness and cunning that hinted at her taste for consensual bondage.

Deirdre stood behind the senator and the movie star, a majordomo near and ready to serve, as Hansen greeted guests who'd paid either because they supported him or because they wanted to meet and visit the home of Barbara Stein. It didn't matter which to Deirdre. The campaign had to raise $250,000 a day to pay for a statewide race in California. The fifty-five-year-old senator exuded an air of maturity and experience. He was dressed in casual attire in a light blue button-down shirt to present himself as approachable and relatable. Light hazel eyes, framed by thin, graying eyebrows, maintained eye contact during interactions, projecting genuine interest.

A woman in an Apolline cropped jacket appeared overcome with emotion and hugged Hansen, patting his back. "God bless you, Senator," she said and moved into the party.

Suddenly, Hansen's engaged expression lost its focus.

Deirdre followed his stricken gaze to the doorway, where a stooped middle-aged man stared at him. The man, dressed in an open-collar shirt and tweed sports jacket, with salt-and-pepper hair pulled into a small ponytail behind his balding pate, joined the receiving line and stood behind three people while Hansen concentrated on the guests before him.

Did he recognize this man? "Get closer," she whispered to Bobby Sutton, her security chief–too late to alert Stein's plainclothes security force.

The ponytailed man squeezed Hansen's hand.

The senator's face blanched, and lines furrowed his everyman's face.

The man beamed and laughed. "Allan, it's about time you invited me to one of your parties."

"Hello, Jake," Hansen said with a feeble smile and pulled his hand free. "Glad you could make it. You a fan of Barbara?" He tried to pass him on to the movie star.

The hostess glanced at the man, who ignored her.

"Sure not your fan," Gillium said with a tight grin.

Hansen shut his eyes as if against a throb of sudden pain and sighed. "Well, it was good…nice…too long not seeing you, Jake."

"You said you wanted to see me, Allan?" Gillium seemed not to care about the others waiting behind him.

"Ah, I need to do my political thing. Talk to Deirdre, she'll take real good care of you."

Hansen's professional politician mask seemed to be shattered by the encounter. He looked at her with a pleading concentration in his fatigue-framed eyes.

The man ignored Deirdre, keeping his attention on Hansen. "I think it's better we talk alone. We have a lot to catch up about, don't you think, Allan?"

"Not here. Deirdre," he said as a command.

"When's a good time?" The man's voice was nasal, insistent.

Hansen recovered his strength. "Good to see you, Jake. We'll talk real soon." He focused on the next person in line. "Nice to see you," he said to an elderly woman.

"Perhaps I can help you." Deirdre put her hand on Gillium's elbow. Something about the power of her touch or the sight of Bobby Sutton, a stoical man with short hair, a flattened nose, and cauliflower wrestler's ears, ready to inflict more pain, allowed her to guide the threat away from the receiving line as if pulling a dog from a fight.

When she had him by the front exit, she turned. "Hi, I'm Senator Hansen's assistant, Deirdre Owens."

Gillium reflexively squeezed her hand, keeping his gaze on Hansen.

"Jake Gillium," he introduced himself with a smirk.

She now understood Hansen's reaction. Deirdre spent as much effort conducting negative research on her candidate as on his opponent. Here was a man that could cause Hansen a lot of trouble.

"What may we do for you, Mr. Gillium?"

"We?" he asked. He had a jolly air, a clown face hiding a tortured soul. "Do you have a mouse in your pocket?" He giggled.

"I mean the senator and his staff."

He looked her up and down. "And a very capable-looking staff at that."

"May I do anything to help you?"

Gillium looked at her as if trying to decide whether to attempt another lame joke, but settled for a drawn-out, "Nooo, I'd better talk to Allan."

"You and the senator are old friends. I recognize your name."

He twisted thin lips. "Wouldn't exactly say friends."

"You were at Cal together, weren't you?"

Gillium harrumphed. "Well, if you know so much, you should know he sent me to jail for seven years with perjured evidence."

Now that she knew the problem, Deirdre could work on the solution. With a nod, she dismissed Bobby Sutton. "Why don't we go outside? I've studied your case. The FBI set you up."

Her apparent agreement caused Gillium to look at her with a turn of his head and narrowed eyes. He walked beside her, apart from the main grouping of guests, around the pool to the seagull sculpture.

"Mr. Gillium, what did you mean when you said you thought the senator wanted to see you?"

"He sent me a note with the invitation."

"Do you have the note with you?"

"I gave it to your people out front. Now, if you'll excuse me, I do want to see what Allan wanted. These surroundings aren't to my taste."

She followed him back into the party.

Gillium stopped. Hansen was no longer in the receiving line. Deirdre mimicked Gillium's scan of the room. Where was he?

They walked past a home theater with plush reclining chairs facing a projection screen. A security guard barred a closed door at the end of the hallway leading to the private area of the house. Gillium turned to Deirdre. "Where did he go?" he demanded.

Trouble came from the front door, where the famous hostess growled at a young blond campaign staffer at the name tag table. The voice Deirdre had heard so many times in songs and movies was furious. Her expressive lips were downturned from her prominent cheekbone. "It better be a fucking national emergency. You get him on the line! I want to talk to him!"

Deirdre hurried to the actress.

Stein's narrowed eyes flashed with anger and a hint of amusement at the odd behavior as if she was delivering a laugh line.

"Where's our boy? He took off like he'd forgotten his wife at the airport. What's going on?"

Deirdre didn't hide her concern. "I believe there was some kind of emergency, a personal emergency." Lying came quickly and easily to Deirdre these days.

"You can tell him that I'm doing this for the party, not him!" Stein spun and left for the guarded door at the end of the hallway.

Gillium chuckled and stayed by Deirdre's side. "Allan's in trouble, isn't he?"

"Why, no. He's very popular, running a fabulous reelection race." Never say a negative thing about your candidate.

"Do you often have to dissemble for Allan?"

Deirdre blinked and tilted her head. "Dissemble? Why, no. I don't know what you mean."

With a tone of an adult lecturing a child, eyes rolled up toward her, bald head bobbing into thick shoulders, he said, "You know what's obvious about you? Lying when you know it's a lie."

Deirdre stiffened. "Will you excuse me?" Lips pressed together; she went out to the driveway. The SUV that had brought them was gone.

She knew when her candidate was losing his/her mind–a bad feeling like seeing your stock drop 50 percent overnight.

Her suitcase and computer were in the SUV Hansen had driven off in. Was she supposed to make her own way to the next event? She hit his name on her cell, and the line went straight to a message. He'd freaked. Her candidate was on the run.

Gillium came up beside her. "Allan was never very courageous, a bit spine deprived, I'm afraid. If you ever track him down, tell him a group doing negative research on him has approached me. They're quite good, really. They've uncovered more than I thought existed in public about Allan's and my relationship with the Oakland Four."

"What did you tell them?"

He handed her a business card. "Tell Allan to call me." He started to walk up the driveway, turned, and said, "You might also want to know that I recognized an FBI agent at your party."

Deirdre squinted in consternation and looked at the card marked with an elaborate depiction of a dam blowing up.

*Jake Gillium*
*editor@permanentecorevolution.org.*

Bobby Sutton came up to her. "What the fuck?" he asked. He was smart as well as tough, SEAL team tough. One of the advantages of running an $80 million campaign was that you could hire good talent.

"This is a setup," Deirdre said. "I want the room swept and facial recognition on every guest. One is FBI."

"On it," Sutton said.

"How long you need on the guests?" Deirdre demanded.

"Ten, no, seven minutes."

"Here." She handed him the card. "I want the address."

Five minutes later, Deirdre stepped up to the microphone set up by the pool where Hansen was to have delivered short remarks. Her voice carried across the property through the PA. "I want to thank you for your support of freedom and the work Senator Allan Hansen is doing in the US Senate." Her voice rose as if announcing an emergency. "We believe this party has been compromised by the senator's political opponents, very likely the White House. I'm going to have to ask everyone to leave so that proper security measures may be taken."

To blame the White House for evicting fifty people who'd paid $1,000 after they'd barely had time to get a drink and a crab canapé was probably not her best move. Still, she had a bad feeling about someone from the FBI inviting Jake Gillium, who most probably was recording their interaction for a hit piece. Whomever it was, she didn't want to give them any more time.

# THREE

## ALLAN HANSEN

The driver was one of the many young people who passed through his staff and campaign, eager to take a first step into politics. At least she'd obeyed the golden rule of drivers and had stayed by the car.

He climbed into the back seat of the SUV and told her to drive him to LA.

Riding in the back and being chauffeured used to seem pretentious. Five years of deferential treatment had changed his attitude and how he played the part of a US senator. Now, he felt like a two-bit actor fleeing the stage in a blind panic.

The driver started the car and drove out of the driveway just as one of the campaign staff came running out the front door.

Hansen leaned back into the seat. He breathed deeply, and his pulse slowed. He'd escaped a trap. Somebody surely had snuck in a camera—no reason for him to stick around and make matters worse. Jake Gillium didn't walk into a fundraiser out of the blue. There was probably already a picture of them circulating on the internet—Allan Hansen with his former Oakland Four coconspirator.

His stomach knotted at the thought of the Berkeley eco-terrorist group. He could beat the charge of being a radical environmentalist in college, but not what he'd done to Jake Gillium.

"Hello, Senator." The driver glanced into the rear view mirror with a worried contraction of her eyes.

Hansen responded with a reflexive, impersonal "Hi." Gillium's joke about being no fan showed he still harbored ill feelings. Why shouldn't he? Hansen's testimony had helped put him and Lauren in jail. But there had been other evidence of their involvement in the attempted firebombing of the Monsanto laboratory. He wasn't the one who'd been charged as an accomplice.

"Where are we going, Senator?"

His phone buzzed, no doubt from his manipulator in chief, Deirdre Owens. He silenced the call.

"Pull in here. There."

Understandably confused, the obedient driver turned into the parking lot of El Matador Beach.

He was rarely harsh with his staff, treating them with the same loco parentis forbearance he'd shown his students before he'd gone into politics. "I need the car," he snapped. "Get out."

He and the bewildered staffer exited the SUV. The sun and hissing of waves were a serene contrast to the panic of a fleeing politician.

"I'm sorry. It's important." Hansen slid behind the wheel, closed the door, and drove out onto the PCH, leaving the young staffer with a befuddled squint to find her own way home with a crazy story of being abandoned by Senator Allan Hansen.

By the time he'd driven through Santa Monica to Interstate 10 East, he'd refused multiple calls from Deirdre Owens and Joe Upton, his chief of staff.

He needed to be alone with memories of innocence and guilt.

———◦⊙◦———

In 1985, near the end of his freshman year at Cal, he'd been nineteen years old, crossing Upper Sproul Plaza to take a final exam in Introduction to Psychology. At six-foot-one, he was taller than most other students, lean, his hair long and parted in the middle. The beginning of a brown beard covered his cheeks and dimpled chin. He wore an army surplus jacket, jeans, and old scuffed hiking boots. He carried his books in a leather satchel slung over a broad shoulder.

"Allan! Allan!" Jake Gillium, his roommate in Stern, ran up to him. Gillium was a Jewish intellectual from Los Angeles and seemed a real sophisticate to someone like Hansen, who'd grown up on an almond farm in the Central Valley.

"Hi, Jake. How ya doing?"

Gillium was out of breath. His wild mass of black curls surrounded a beard that Hansen envied. Gillium's dark eyes searched the crowd before settling on Hansen.

"Not so good." Gillium gave a nervous laugh that heightened his air of panic. His eyes beneath thick black eyebrows darted about, then focused on him with a look of pleading. "Look, we were studying for exams last night, right?"

They had been alone in their dorm room studying when Gillium had left around nine, saying he had to give a ride to an older couple they had met at Revolution Books. Hansen had thought it odd that they needed a ride somewhere at that time of night but was more focused on preparing for today's exam and hadn't asked why.

Gillium passionately believed in the need for social change and to stop environmental destruction. He had led Hansen to the apartment of Jimmy Tolver and his beautiful redheaded companion Lauren Bastini, saying they were *real revolutionaries*.

Tolver hypnotized Hansen with his charm and spoke to him as an equal, not a young kid. Weaving quotes from environmental leaders, he spoke admirably about the sixties radicals and their resistance to the Vietnam War. He'd given Hansen a copy of the Edward Abbey book *The Monkey Wrench Game*, in which an older protagonist led young followers around the Southwest, mostly blowing up power lines. Hansen saw his sexual relationship with Bastini reflected in the book.

Being seduced by a thirty-six-year-old woman had seemed impossibly exotic and sophisticated. If she'd been talking about monkeys, he'd have agreed with her to see the way her nipples swelled and the slope of her belly.

Gillium's eyes focused on something in the plaza, and he took off at a run, his short legs and thin arms pumping, his open plaid shirt flapping behind him.

Four men in dark sunglasses and suits chased Gillium through the crowd.

Hansen saw two men dressed in suits angling toward him. He broke into a fast walk as they closed on him.

"Allan Hansen?"

He lurched forward and stopped.

"Willard Mastroni, FBI," the man claimed but showed no badge. "We have a warrant for your arrest."

Hansen nervously pushed his hair away from his face. If he ran, it would only add to their suspicion. He swallowed against the tightening pressure in his throat. He hadn't done anything. "There must be a mistake. I haven't done anything and . . . I have a test. I can't . . ."

"Come with us." They moved to either side of him.

"What do you want?" His voice cracked in his dry throat. Sweat broke out on his forehead.

They held him by his trembling arm to hurry him across the plaza.

His feet dragged, and he almost tripped. He righted himself and moved faster to keep up with them. "Can you please just tell me what's this all about?"

Neither of them responded.

Near the low oval wall around Ludwig's Fountain, Gillium was spread-eagle on the ground. Two men held him down while another handcuffed him. A pistol was aimed at Gillium's head. An excited, shocked crowd was gathering around the scene. Hansen looked away from students' stares as the FBI agents hustled him past the Free Speech Movement Monument to a car waiting on Bancroft.

As they roughly guided Hansen into the back of a black sedan, a sidewalk preacher cried, "Awaken, arise Israel. Come forth, Babylon. Repent,

repent for the Kingdom."

The drive to the federal building in Oakland was an agony of unanswered questions. Hansen tried to be friendly but could get nothing out of the stolid FBI agents.

He was left alone in a small windowless room that smelled of sweat, tobacco, and fear. A single light shone on a metal desk and three hardback chairs. Thoughts flooded with scenarios, excuses, and lies he could tell to get out of this.

The door opened. Three men entered. Hansen rose to his feet, eyes searching from face to face for a sign of compassion.

"Sit back down, Allan," a man said, pointing at the chair from which Hansen had risen.

He was Japanese like many of Hansen's friends in the Valley. There was something potentially friendly in the laugh creases at the side of his eyes, but Hansen could find nothing understanding in his expression.

The two bigger men stood over Hansen's shoulders.

"I'm Lawrence Yushima, assistant United States attorney for the Northern District of California. These gentlemen are with the FBI.

"Hello, sir. I'm Allan Hansen." He extended his hand with a winsome smile as if introducing himself to a professor.

Yushima did not shake Hansen's hand. "We know who you are, Allan."

Hansen hunched into a position of submission and stammered, "Wh-wh-what can I do for you, sir?"

Yushima opened a manila file on the table and looked at Hansen through the thick lenses of black-rimmed glasses. "I want you to tell me about the plot to firebomb the Monsanto biotech research facility on Dwight Way."

Hansen couldn't stop a shiver that spread through his hands. "I don't know anything about it. I swear I don't."

"You know James Tolver and Lauren Bastini." It wasn't a question but a statement of fact.

"Yes, sir. I've met them a few times."

"James Tolver has died, and Lauren Bastini has suffered serious injuries received while attempting last night at approximately 9:45 p.m. to plant a bomb at the Monsanto biotech research facility."

Time seemed to momentarily stop. His entire being was thrust into a disoriented realm of disbelief. "No! I'm sorry, I mean . . ."

"Were you present at any discussions between Jacob Gillium and Lauren Bastini about attacking the Monsanto biotech research facility?"

His mind raced, desperately trying to catch up with what was happening to him. He was having a hard time speaking. His words either sounded like they were coming out in a rush or not fast enough. His heart was racing like he had touched an electric current.

"No, sir."

"Were you present when there were any discussions about the sabotage of environmentally damaging activities?"

"Maybe a couple of times, but I didn't think anybody was serious."

"Serious about what?" The US attorney's voice was calm, leading.

Hansen shook his head, feeling lost, helpless to find the words to save his life. "You know, revolution. Everybody, I mean lots of people, talk that way about defending the environment. You know trees and things, redwood forests."

Yushima frowned and glanced over Hansen's shoulders at the FBI agents.

"You talk that way, Allan?"

Hansen leaned forward, shaking his head, squinting in sincerity. "No."

Yushima opened the file. "You ever say, 'I know where we can get some blasting caps'?"

Hansen's hands twitched on the table. He put them in his lap. His eyes flitted. He'd been with Gillium at Lauren's apartment, sitting around a low table in a living room cluttered with old furniture, a bike in the hallway, and stacks of books. An Alfred Eisenstaedt poster of Rachel Carson sitting by a rock pool as if contemplating the destruction of the natural world she foresaw hung on the wall. Lauren, Jimmy Tolver, and Cliffy were there. They had been talking about where to get some explosives. Hansen had just

19

been showing off. He'd made up a story about an uncle with a gold mine.

"I was just kidding, really." He sounded like he was gagging.

The federal prosecutor succinctly stated the indictment. "Allan, we have photographs of you at planning meetings. We have an informant who will testify that you were a coconspirator. Do you know what that means? It means that we can prosecute you for any crimes James Tolver, Lauren Bastini, and Jacob Gillium planned or committed. Last night, they were attempting to ignite a gas bomb. They could have burned down half of Oakland. And you would have been responsible." Yushima jabbed a finger at Hansen. "You are responsible for the death of James Tolver. Mr. Hansen, I have enough evidence to charge you with felony murder."

Hansen rocked back in his seat as if shoved by a powerful hand.

"Murder! I didn't do anything. I swear to God, I didn't! I wouldn't know what a blasting cap looked like if I saw one. I was just talking, I tell you!"

Yushima calmly stared at him, utterly unimpressed by his denial. "You were with Jacob Gillium last night."

Jake had gotten him into this—Jake and his damn free-love save-the-planet crowd. He wished he'd never met Jake Gillium.

Yushima leaned over the table toward him. "If you knew the crime Tolver, Bastini, and Gillium were attempting and you did nothing to stop them, you are guilty of conspiracy to commit the crime. You are an accessory before the fact."

Hansen slowly shook his head. His mouth hung open. He wanted to wake up from this nightmare. What could he do or say to make this man believe he was innocent, completely innocent?

"Did you know that Jacob Gillium drove Lauren Bastini and James Tolver last night to attack the Monsanto facility?"

Hansen looked at the thick folder that now seemed to hold every crazy word he'd ever said or heard. Did they know that he'd made love to Lauren? He'd bragged about it to Jake. How many of Gillium's revolutionary rants or insane schemes were in there–things Hansen had listened to or expressed agreement with? He tried to swallow what felt like a knot of rags clogging his throat. "He spoke about genetically modified seeds." Hansen raised his palms toward Yushima, pleading, trying to make him comprehend what it was like to be a student at Cal. "You have to understand, sir. Lots of students talk that way about defending the environment. We have classes where we talk that way."

"Whose idea was it to attack the facility? Was it Jacob Gillium's?" There was no understanding, no sympathy in Yushima's voice or expression.

Maybe Jake had known something about the bombing. He did say last night he was going to drive them, but he hadn't said where. "I don't know. I don't think so. I never heard Jake say anything like that."

Yushima leaned back and frowned to convey his displeasure with Hansen's statements. "Let me explain this simply to you, Mr. Hansen. Here are the scenarios. You can join Lauren Bastini and Jacob Gillium in prison for a very long time, or you can be our witness and testify as to what Gillium and Bastini said and did."

"Jesus! It was just talk. I never gave anyone any blasting caps. I never told anyone where they could find blasting caps. Jake was studying in our dorm room last night. He's a good student. He wouldn't hurt anyone. He likes to talk. He's a big talker!"

Yushima's stare made Hansen cringe and fall back into his chair. The attorney leaned toward him. "I'm giving you one chance. You will testify against Jacob Gillium and Lauren Bastini, or you will join them in prison."

Hansen started to sob, melting inside, his body flowing from his eyes. "I didn't do anything. Jake didn't do anything. We use Monsanto on my family's farm. I spray Roundup myself."

Yushima looked up at the agents. "I think Mr. Hansen had better get used to being behind bars. Book him."

He thought about his mother hearing about him sleeping with a thirty-five-year-old revolutionary. "Wait!" He wept and held up his hands.

The agents and federal attorney watched him.

"I guess Jake did know that Lauren was going to do something. If I had known what he knew about it, I would have told someone."

Yushima smiled as if he was proud of him. "And when did Jake first discuss the plan to attack the Monsanto biotech research facility?"

———◦◉◦———

He'd testified that Jake had said he was going to drive Bastini and Tolver somewhere. Jake hadn't said where. Jake's lawyer had said Jake had been told the gas can was to start a car that had run out of gas, that he'd left them off a block away from the Monsanto facility and had driven away.

The FBI informant, Cliffy, had testified that Jake had been present at planning sessions for ecoterrorism activities. So had Hansen. He was the unidentified fourth conspirator of the Oakland Four. It was pointless saying he and Jake wanted to impress Tolver and Bastini, to be accepted by them. Hansen knew he would have driven them. Everything he'd been able to do with his life, to be a US senator, was because Jake had a car and he didn't.

# FOUR

## JAKE GILLIUM

Deirdre was getting into a staff car in Stein's driveway when she took the call from Joe Upton, the senator's chief of staff.

Upton lived and breathed Allan Hansen, a codependent relationship that extended to his habitual referral to "we" when talking about him.

"What's going on? Where's the senator?" he asked, as panicked as if he'd lost his child.

He must not have been able to reach him any more than she had. "You'll have to ask him that."

"I hear you shut down the event, blamed the White House for what? What the hell is going on?"

He must have had a plant at the party. Deirdre bet it was the blonde at the door.

"I think they set a trap for Allan."

"Why? What makes you think that? Has everybody out there lost their minds?"

"Somebody sent Jacob Gillium an invitation. You know the Oakland Four?"

"Oh."

That shut him up for a minute.

"I have information it was the FBI. We found bugs. We're running facial scans."

"Oh, sweet Jesus, this is getting dirty."

*Getting dirty? What Pollyanna world do you live in?*

"I've got to go. Call me if you reach Allan," she said.

"Unless you have something solid, please keep it quiet, and let's use it in our own way and time."

What time was that? After everyone who wanted to be senator got into the race.

"I don't need you telling me how to run a campaign."

"Look, you work for us. Do what we tell you."

She hung up on the toad.

———◦◉◦———

The next morning, she picked up a rental car at LAX and headed up Fairfax Avenue.

Her phone rang with a tone she knew was the senator.

"Morning, Deirdre." He sounded raring to go.

"Senator." She matched his chipper tone as if nothing had happened last night.

"What do we got this morning?"

"You're in your Santa Monica office, meeting the mayor for a walk-through Koreatown at ten o'clock. Eleven to noon, you're dialing for dollars. The call sheet is in your daily file."

She knew he hated fundraising–most politicians did–so he raised a topic he hated more. "Sorry about last night. I drove off with your clothes."

"That's all right. I got around."

"You went to the dinner?"

"Yes, we raised $50 K."

"Good for you."

Three of the dinner party were happy to get home to their families. She mollified the fourth by drinking with him and maxed his contribution by taking him back to her hotel room. He'd been OK, lousy really, but most drunks were, especially older men. What did she expect? Her present lover, Paul Barstow, was ten years younger than her, and he liked it rough.

"Jake Gillium have anything to say?" Hansen finally asked.

"Not really. You know it was a setup. We found his invitation with a handwritten note, supposedly from you, inviting him. Bobby Sutton found microphones with an RF detector. We're doing facial-scan recognition, trying to pick up the planter. I think it may have been FBI, that woman who hugged you. You should discard that shirt you were wearing."

Hansen humphed. "I heard you called the White House out."

"I don't think the FBI would be doing this on their own."

"You're probably right, but without proof, we don't want to sound paranoid."

She bet he'd already been talking to Upton. "It's not paranoia when someone *is* bugging your fundraiser."

"Yes, you're right," he said. "It's just the right-wing media crowd are going to town on it. They love it happened at Barbara Stein's. She's a favorite liberal bugaboo."

"You're going to be asked about it. Might as well back me," Deirdre said.

"I'll think about it."

"I know you'll make the right decision. Blame me if you want. You're the one whose name is on the ballot, not me."

His voice went deeper. "You know about Jake and me?"

"Of course. We've been through your past. So has the opposition. You've got nothing to hide. Senator, you saved lives by going undercover for the government."

"Is that what we're saying?"

"That's what I say."

"I guess it's the best spin."

"It's not spin. You're a hero."

"Yeah, sure."

She joined his chuckle. "Just doing my job."

"You have any way of getting in touch with Jake, maybe arrange something quiet where we can get together?"

"I'm on it."

"Damn, you're good."

"So are you, Senator, an American hero I'm honored to serve."

"Throw back my shoulders and walk the walk."

"That's it."

"I about quit last night," he said.

"So did I."

He chuckled. "Glad you didn't. I needed a breather, that's all. I stayed at my brother's in Redlands. He was out of town, had the place to myself. It was just what I needed."

"Do call Barbara Stein. I calmed her down. She got it once we found the bugs. She said she walked off herself with a full feature film crew waiting. I'll text you her number. Lot of people depend on you. A lot at stake in this election. That's why we're going to win."

"Maybe."

"I'm going to fight for it."

"Guess I should too."

"It's worth it."

"I'll call Barbara."

"OK. I'll try to catch up with you at the Wilshire."

*Politics ain't beanbag*, the aphorism goes. Not for the first time, she thought her candidate was too nice for the job. Maybe it was his innate goodness that created his bond with voters, why he succeeded when other more ruthless candidates failed. Sincerity had always been his shtick—why she'd picked him.

Deirdre was the middle child of Irish immigrants who worked hard on a small plot of land to survive. Her brothers protected her from outside the family but not from each other. She fought with them just as they fought with each other.

She'd grown up in the country, slitting the throat to bleed a buck she'd shot. Maybe she'd gotten into politics and was good at it because she knew how to hunt, how to kill. She wasn't nice, never had the patience for playing with the girls, and the boys didn't like a woman tougher than they were. Might be why she was into the BDSM game, where the bottom understood that she was the top, the dom.

She had the radio tuned to a college FM station playing National Public Radio morning news. All the reporters had the same slightly left bias and spoke in calm tones as if an antidote to the hysteria of commercial news and commentary. The piece was on Alex Uberhoff, the new director of the Office of National Intelligence, a New York corporator raider who'd been brought in to coordinate the myriad US government spy agencies.

The piece reminded her she had a date with Paul Barstow when she got back to DC. She'd met Paul in a kickboxing class. The way he'd said, "Don't hurt me," had given her the clue that they might have another interest in common. She was right. He liked the consensual nonconsensual game where he'd act as if he wasn't enjoying the unpleasant things she did to him in bed–even if he did.

Barstow was angling for a political appointment in the ODNI–not a hard reach since anybody with any pride would never work in this administration.

She was taking a chance by being his playmate. But hard to pass on a partner who shared her particular tastes in body if not politics.

She navigated the twisted spaghetti freeway exchange between the 5 and 101 onto the 60 and got off on Whittier Boulevard. Boyle Heights was a mix of Victorian-era homes, Art Deco buildings, murals, street art, and storefronts. Haphazardly painted hieroglyphs of graffiti-covered walls and the sides of houses that looked sacked and abandoned situated beside well-tended homes and yards. Sharp stalks of birds of paradise with their orange and purple beaks were planted at the edges of yards with old wooden fences and porch poles interlaced with fiery red bougainvillea.

Signs in Korean and Spanish marked small stores. A Black woman led two small children down the sidewalk. Men in trucks loaded with gardening equipment drove by. Latinas in hotel maid uniforms waited at a bus stop.

The address Bobby had found, 1543 ½ Laster Road, was probably easy enough to find at the site registration, but Bobby had other channels, nowhere near what the bastards in the White House had. Nobody ever accused them of playing fair.

A sign reading *Gillium Grocery and Sundries* hung across two picture windows plastered with advertisements. Drawn white blinds covered the windows on the second floor of the tan brick building.

Eating a pastry and carrying a Styrofoam cup, a man came out the open front door.

Five head-shaved Latino teenagers, dressed in Pendleton wool jackets to be cast off when the heat rose, watched her pull to the curb. Hot bunking—not their turn to sleep—put them out on the street so early in the morning. With the rental car and business suit, she was an attraction, something new. She stood out. They sauntered down the block toward her.

Drinks were illuminated in coolers on one side of the darkened store. Three aisles lined with shelves of cans and bottles led to a meat section in the back.

A woman with a flower-print dress and a spangled scarf tied over one shoulder sat behind a cash register. Rings on each finger and three bands of bracelets hung from her left wrist. Leather pierced by two wooden skewers held her red-tinted ponytail. A thrusting jaw beneath magenta-coated lips indicated a never-say-die spirit, ready to stand up to the next blow, get back up, and fight again.

"Hi. I'm looking for 1543 ½ Laster," Deirdre asked her.

The woman's attitude went from professional courtesy to suspicion. She put down the *Los Angeles Times* Metro section and studied Deirdre through bright eyes capped by green eyeshadow. "There is no such address."

Her accent had a trace of Yiddish.

The bangers went to coolers behind Deirdre. The woman did not move her gaze from Deirdre.

"I was trying to find Jake Gillium. He told me I might find him at this address."

"Let me see," the woman said.

Deirdre passed the card to her.

The gypsy-looking woman studied it as if to see if it was authentic.

One of the *vatos* stepped up beside Deirdre and set a container of chocolate milk and a package of white donuts on the worn Formica counter. "Hey, Mizz G," he said.

Mizz G took his money.

The others brought her similar sugar-laden purchases.

One of them looked Deirdre up and down.

She returned his stare with an unwavering gaze, not flinching or stepping away when they surrounded her. If he only knew what she would do with him in bed.

"Yo?" he asked. "What you, a lawyer?"

She laughed quickly. "Nah, *politica*."

They nodded and went back to their stations on the street.

"I don't know this address."

"I met Jake last night."

Fury broke through Mizz G's control. "With Allan Hansen?" Her face reddened beneath the tan foundation, and dark pupils flashed anger. "My son has nothing to say to Allan Hansen."

*With good reason*, Deirdre thought. "I think he'd want to hear what I have to say."

"Hansen is a liar."

"Mama!"

Deirdre peered into the gloom of the store to see Gillium setting down a dolly piled with cardboard boxes. She turned from the glowering woman and stepped back from the counter.

He was dressed in black jeans and a short-sleeved green shirt with two golf clubs crossed on a coat of arms on his left breast.

"Jake." She held out her hand.

"You haven't changed your clothes. Been up all night?" he asked, eyes rolling up from his lowered head as if sly.

"Hazards of the job, but I was pleasantly fucked last night. How about you?"

He bent as she suspected he would before her power. His laughter overcame his resistance.

"Don't talk to her," his mother warned.

"All right, Mama." His voice was sweet with concern for her.

"You come to fuck me?" he asked Deirdre.

"Jacob!" Mizz G exclaimed.

Deirdre and Jake smiled at each other like two kids caught misbehaving.

A man with a cane maneuvered around them and placed a can of condensed milk on the counter. His hand was snaked with veins and wrinkled skin worn by a life of hard labor.

Deirdre turned her back to the customer and faced Gillium. "I wanted to speak to you about what you said last night about people contacting you about Allan."

Gillium's focus sharpened, and he raised his head to look more directly at her. "I went to that bourgeois palace of bad taste to speak to Allan. I've been trying for years."

Deirdre sighed. Here was the legislative side pushing into the political. "How have you tried to reach him?"

"How is a constituent supposed to reach his representative? I called his office. Went to his office. Wrote. Nothing."

"That is wrong, seriously wrong."

"Can you do something about it?"

"Damn skippy."

Gillium was visibly warming to her. "Tell him I consider him a fellow comrade."

"Can we word it a bit differently?" Deirdre broke a laugh that had been waiting since last night.

Gillium joined her, and the ice was broken.

"I have got a token of peace for him. Come on, I'll show you." Gillium turned toward the rear of the store.

Mizz G pressed her painted lips together and shook her head.

Deirdre followed him through a storage room out a rear door.

A cement walkway led to a rear house. Canna lilies grew along a wooden fence.

He opened a screen door to a room walled with bookshelves. A long desk with a computer and telephone faced a window. Gillium picked up a remote control and turned off a television set tuned to MSNBC. Rows of records and stacks of CDs filled every conceivable space. An unmade bed was visible down a short hallway in a smaller rear room.

Did he really think she'd come to fuck him? She liked him. In another time or place, she might. One fuck for the job was her limit, and that had been expended last night.

"How old is your mother? She's amazing looking."

"Seventy-nine. Still going strong and sharp as a tack."

"You look like you're doing all right yourself."

"Allan and I are the same age. We were college roommates, you know. Here's a picture of us when we were young."

He handed Deirdre a color photo of two fresh-faced teenagers, a man, and a woman, with her hand thrust forward, holding five bundled eighteen-inch sticks of dynamite with a timer attached to the middle. Deirdre focused on the image of the woman. Curly red hair framed a round face with a deadly serious expression in narrowed eyes and pressed lips.

Hansen looked up from his lowered gaze with a bemused expression, as if asking, *Can you believe this?*

"I found this the other day. It's me, Allan, Jimmy Tolver, and Lauren Bastini—the Oakland Four, some would say."

The fourth member of the Oakland Four remained a mystery. Had it been Allan Hansen? Their opposition would certainly say so. Deirdre hurriedly put the picture in her jacket pocket. "You know," she said. "I wasn't

31

shitting you. I studied your case. Allan is obsessed with it. Everything he's doing in the Senate, why he's running, is to stop this from doing to anyone they want what they did to you. It was FBI, a COINTELPRO operation."

"Yeah, they're back at it. I recognized an agent last night. Cliffy. His real name is George Blum. I've followed his career. You don't lose interest in a man who ruined your life."

"If they win this seat and take back the Senate, no one will be able to stop them."

"And you think Allan will stop them?"

"He has every reason to, and you have every reason to help."

Gillium huffed a quick laugh. "You ever stop dissembling?"

"When I want," she pouted.

"I'd like to see more of you, the real you."

He stepped closer and took her hand. His eyes were large for his face, with irises like black olives.

She was a sucker for sincerity and looked at him without blinking. "I don't want to see what happened to you happen to anyone else. With today's technology, we're a cooperating Congress away from a nightmare surveillance state."

He released her hand and stepped back. "All business, are we?" He shook his head with a mixture of disgust and sadness. "Like we're not already there?"

"Close but not complete. That's why they're after Allan so hard."

Gillium shrugged and, in a voice that didn't completely hide his lasting anger, said, "Some people Allan and I fell in with tried to destroy a lab of a company they thought profited from environmental destruction. It was a setup. The police were waiting for them. Jimmy Tolver and Lauren Bastini allegedly resisted arrest. The police fired twenty-two rounds at them. Both were shot. Jimmy died. Lauren survived but was severely burned when the gas can exploded. Allan and I both knew them. We were both studying for exams when it happened. He gets to be a senator, and I get . . ." He held up his hands, looked around his cottage, and shrugged. He smiled at her. "Enough self-pity. I was an idiot to drive them. I thought I saw something in you. Was I wrong?"

"Maybe not. I hope not, but I'm serious about the importance of having Allan in the Senate. I have a job to do."

"And I have a store to run." He led her out of his house.

When they reentered, Mizz G stood up and came around the counter. "I need to go upstairs. You mind the cash register."

"Go ahead, Mama. I have it."

Mizz G walked by them, shifting her eyes as she passed Deirdre. "Allan Hansen is a Benedict Arnold," she said, her mouth contorted with hatred.

Gillium cocked his head and smiled as though she were the child and he the adult. "She doesn't really know him, Mama. Deirdre is someone I think you'd like."

"Humph." Mizz G sneered and opened a door to a stairway leading upstairs.

Gillium moved behind the cash register. "My father started this store. I grew up here. He was shot . . . up there." He pointed toward the front door. "They never caught the killer."

Death and murder ripped open a life. What could she do but look sympathetic? Nobody she knew or loved had ever been murdered.

"I was the big hope, you know, the only Jewish son, supposed to be a lawyer, a mensch. When things didn't work out for me like Mom planned, she got a little bitter. But she means something to this community. Everybody knows Mizz G." He spoke with a wistful glance toward the vibrant neighborhood. "Sometimes lives play out on a smaller stage."

"Can you tell me a bit more about the people who have contacted you concerning Allan?"

Gillium pushed himself erect. His head rose. "Tell me, my darling Deirdre, in this climate of fear, how do you think a man who publicly advocates for resistance to environmental destruction and is a convicted terrorist, as some would describe me, tell me—how do you think I am viewed by our government?" He slapped the counter. "I am followed. My friends, my mother, for God's sake, is harassed. My phone is bugged. My mail is opened. Who do you think is after me to betray Allan?" His voice rose. "Let him come down here and stand by my side. Let him stand beside the people driven from their land by environmental destruction and global warming, their small farms made unsustainable by US support of large agribusiness. Let him come down here and defend himself and us against our own government."

Deirdre's arms instinctively crossed in a defensive position. "I know it's the White House who is behind this. We should work together. I need proof. Something that I can show the world."

"As a wise man once said, if it looks like shit, smells like shit, it probably is shit."

They stared into each other's eyes, and she gently smiled. "Want my number?"

"Yeah. I would."

She took out a business card identifying her as *Director, Allan Hansen for Senate*, turned it over, and wrote her personal number on the back."

"I'll make sure Allan knows about your concerns. I'm sure he'll be contacting you soon," she said.

# FIVE

## BAD BUSINESS

Blum waited until closing when no customers appeared in Gillium Grocery and Sundries. He walked in wearing a loose-fitting dark blue suit.

"I think I can help you with the FBI," he addressed Gillium across the counter without a greeting or introduction.

He watched Gillium's glowering eyes blink, and the set of his jaw soften—a glimmer of hope playing across his rigid expression.

"I know you." Gillium reached under the counter at the cash register.

Blum placed both of his hands on the glass surface and leaned forward. "I'm a friend. A friend who can get the FBI off your ass."

Gillium's face swelled red with rage. "Back to ruin more lives, hmm, Cliffy?"

Blum had counted on Gillium not recognizing him. He glanced up at the surveillance camera. Twenty agencies might have the place bugged. "Is there someplace we can talk?" he asked.

He didn't expect what happened next and surely could never have anticipated what followed.

Gillium snapped, all right. The years in jail, his failed dreams for his life, and the injustices seemed to explode out of him in a scream, a venting of fury focused on Blum.

With rage-induced agility, Gillium planted his hands on the counter top and swung his legs over, knocking off a display of jerky and sending a glass jar of pickles crashing to the ground. Before Blum could escape, Gillium's hands were around his neck.

It had been fifteen years since Blum had taken defensive tactics. Instinctively, his fists shot up between his assailant's outstretched arms.

A woman screamed.

Out of the edge of Blum's vision, he saw Gillium's mother aiming a black handgun at him.

Blum reached out and snapped his fist into Gillium's face, sending him back against a candy rack. He frantically tried to pull his .38 Special from his waist holster.

Mizz G's pistol resounded just at the moment Gillium threw himself back at Blum. With audible thumps, the man caught the slugs aimed for him. Gillium's blood splattered into Blum's white dress shirt as he fell into his arms. In all his years with the FBI, Blum had never seen a man shot. Stunned, he held on to the dead weight of the mortally wounded Jake Gillium, whose face was frozen in surprise.

"Jacob!" The agony in the mother's voice would stay with Blum forever.

Blum fell back, and the corpse dropped to the ground. He spun and ran out of the store just as a teenage boy was coming in. Blum dodged past him, bumping into a grizzly bearded wino who stared at him through reddened eyes.

The bum's stinking breath filled Blum's nose as he ran for his car.

Witnesses. Bad business. A real cluster fuck!

———— ✦ ————

The crime lab had finished. The coroner had taken the body. Lieutenant Cork Johnson, a six-foot Black man, lean except for a beer-distended belly, rested his hand on his hip as he addressed the lead detective. "You sure about this description?" he asked.

Michelle Chang's ponytail bobbed as she nodded and pointed to a small camera installed on top of a cooler. "We have it on a twenty-four-hour tape." Her laptop computer was open next to the register. She had already downloaded the security camera feed into an evidence-collecting system at Los Angeles PD.

Johnson watched the stop-action sequence of two men struggling on the computer screen. Even if a family member had done the shooting, if the original perpetrator had started the fight, he could still be up for felony murder.

He saw someone talking and then the victim jumping over the counter. No gun, no threat. There was no crime in talking unless the man had threatened Gillium with robbery, and there was no evidence of that. And an old, fat, well-dressed white man hardly fit the profile of a robber.

"Two witnesses saw him," she said, smiling. "Got good corroborating descriptions from both."

"Any leads?" Johnson asked. He looked toward Detective Larry Gerse, who was recording the homicide scene with a digital movie camera.

Chang glanced at Gerse, hesitated until he was a step closer, and said in a matter-of-fact voice, "She said that the man was working for Allan Hansen."

"Who?" Johnson's wide-set eyes narrowed in suspicion that he was being set up for something.

"The senator," Gerse said.

"What are you telling me?" Johnson snarled. He was not in a joking mood. He worked on a homicide assembly line. If you didn't catch them in the first forty-eight hours, you moved on to the next case. At least with a white perp, you might get some cooperating witnesses. Two white men fight, and one gets shot, more of a case of man biting dog in this neighborhood. Though if a senator was involved, the system would go a 100 percent and then some, no quickly moving on from this case.

Chang looked over at her laptop and then back to Johnson. "The shooter, the mother, says that Senator Hansen had it in for her son. Says the victim had information that would cost Hansen the election, so he sends someone down here to threaten her son. They fight, and the mother accidentally shoots her son. Looks like a pretty clear case of self-defense. We might be able to get enough causation for a second degree or manslaughter on the white intruder."

Johnson held up his two large hands. "Tell me you don't have physical evidence tying Hansen to the crime scene."

Chang and Gerse again exchanged glances. "We may have," Chang said. "We found a name and number in the victim's pocket. The mother said that a woman from Hansen's office had been in the store talking to the victim this morning."

"A woman, not a man. That's not much of a connection. Have you tried to contact her?" Johnson asked.

"No. I'm just finishing with my crime scene report," Chang said.

"Got the number?" Johnson asked.

Chang handed him a clear plastic bag. Visible inside was a business card.

Johnson held it up to the light of a ceiling bulb and read the name, *Deirdre Owens, Senator Hansen*. He pulled out a phone from his pocket and dialed the number on the back of the card.

---

Deirdre was in a hotel in Sacramento, towel wrapped around her waist, wet hair dripping down her back, washing her panties in the sink when her cellphone rang. She dried her hands and went into the bedroom. The LED window on the cellphone displayed a 310 area code.

The voice on the other end of the call had the vestige of a Southern drawl. "Deirdre Owens?"

"Who's calling?"

"Detective Cork Johnson, Los Angeles Police Department. Are you acquainted with Jacob Gillium?"

She exhaled deeply, relieved, followed by renewed concern. "May I ask what this is about?"

"Miss Owens, do you work for Senator Allan Hansen?"

"What is this in reference to?"

"A homicide investigation. Jacob Gillium was shot dead while struggling with an unidentified man this evening in his store. We found your name in Mr. Gillium's pocket."

She shuddered and crossed her arms across her bare chest.

"Miss Owens, did you visit Mr. Gillium in his store yesterday?"

"Yes." She tried to force her thoughts past Gilliam's death.

"What did you and Mr. Gillium talk about?" the policeman asked.

She stalled for time. "What happened?"

Johnson briefly told her the details. Shot by his mother in the same spot where his father had died. Horrible. "What were you discussing with Mr. Gillium?"

The towel had come loose around her waist. Deirdre stood, and it fell to the floor. "He wanted the senator to come visit his neighborhood. I believe Mr. Gillium is . . . was a neighborhood activist."

"Did anybody representing the senator visit Mr. Gillium this evening?"

"No, I don't believe so. What makes you think that anyone associated with Senator Hansen would be involved?"

"His mother is saying she shot at a man that Senator Hansen sent to intimidate her son. The victim was struggling with a white male in a suit when he was shot. Would you have any idea who this man might be?"

She felt the campaign collapsing. If Mizz G was blaming the senator for her shooting her own son, no matter how unlikely, Fox would run with it like a bitch in heat. *Stay cool, stay cool*, she told herself. "Is there any evidence?"

"Surveillance video."

"Then you should be able to identify the man. I'd be happy to view the tape. Have campaign security review the tape."

"Thank you very much. I may have to call you for just that purpose."

She looked at her cell to call Bobby Sutton. Her hand was shaking. A deep sob rose from her chest, a cry for Gillium, for Mizz G, the sudden removal from life, murder, how fragile were those moments when Deidre had seen him alive.

———◦———

Cork Johnson's handheld buzzed. He stared into the cooler of soft drinks as he listened to his captain's voice. "Got it," Johnson said. He furrowed his eyebrows, and scanned the room. "Everybody out," he announced to the two detectives.

"What's up, Cork?" Gerse asked.

"Feds' show now. Don't touch anything else. Get your gear and clear out. Set up some barrier tape. Nobody touches anything until they get here."

"What about the surveillance tape?" Gerse asked.

Johnson hesitated an instant. Something wasn't right about this. "Leave it for the Homeland Security," he said.

———◦———

"Get down to LAPD," Deirdre instructed Bobby Sutton. "See if you can look at the tape. Take something to record what you see; doubt they would give you a copy."

"Not likely. I got a lapel pin I can use. Want me to do something about the mom?"

The question held the heavy water weight of implication. What did *something about the mom* mean? Silence her? Bribe her? Reason with her? Were they going to start playing dirty like the White House?

"No, the senator would never approve of anything like that. It's his campaign. The voters are just going to have to trust him and not Mizz G. She has every right to be hysterical." Deirdre's voice caught. "Poor woman."

"Yeah, shot her own son. That's wrong."

"So wrong. Got to do some damage control. Let's find out who Gillium was fighting with."

"On it."

Next, she called Upton. He might be a self-important flunky, but the senator listened to him. She would need him to keep Hansen in the race. From the sound of Upton's voice, she knew she'd awoken him.

"Got to talk to you," she said.

"I'll call you back from my study," he said.

Two minutes later, she briefed him on the Gillium story.

"Have you told the senator?" Upton asked.

"No, I need your help to calm him down. You whisper in one ear and me the other. Tell him he had nothing to do with this tragedy."

"Think he'll go for that?" Upton asked.

Deirdre pressed her lips together and blinked. "He's got to get over it. What happened to those people wasn't his fault."

"We talking about the same guy? He feels things. He's an empath."

Deirdre sighed. "I know. At least let's get our press lined up. Terrible tragedy, deepest sympathies. Prayers are with the family and friends."

"Sure, sure. Thanks for ruining my night."

"Got to share the pain."

"You're good at that."

Deirdre gritted her teeth. "Meaning?" She put a knife in the question.

Upton exhaled. "It's nearly two here. I've got a lot on my plate."

"You got something to say to me, say it."

"Not now."

"You little mealy mouth son of a bitch. Just push your paper and leave the campaign alone." Her voice trembled with rage.

"You're the campaign?" he mocked her.

"Damn close to it. It's me, or he quits."

Upton lost it. "I get asked about you. You've got quite a story. Just don't be the reason he quits."

With a bitter laugh, she said, "There's a crowded shelf teetering over this campaign."

"Well, don't knock into it. One of us has to call him. He watches the news all night."

"They'll save it for the morning news. Better let me talk to him. He's just down the hall. I'll go to his room."

The tension left Upton's voice, calm now, off the hook. "All right, call me if you need me. I won't bring it up unless he does. Now, I'm going to take my Ambien and try and get two hours of sleep."

"Love you, babe."

"You are such a what-I-can't-call-you. I know you'll do it right."

Deirdre redressed in the clothes she'd been wearing for two days. Her suitcase was still in Los Angeles. She'd be home in San Francisco tomorrow and could reload.

She left the wet panties hanging off the shower curtain rod and walked down the hallway.

More mental health counselor than a political strategist, Deirdre knocked on Hansen's hotel door.

She heard him moving to the door and sensed him looking through the peephole.

He opened the door enough so he could look out but not reveal his body.

"I have some bad news," she said.

His head rocked back, eyes narrowed with apprehension that someone in his family was dead or injured.

"It's Jake Gillium. He's dead."

Hansen huffed, unclear if by concern or relief.

"Let me put on some pants," he said, moving toward the closet.

"Don't have to for me," Deirdre said, stepping into the room, closing the door behind her.

"What happened to Jake?" He stood at the foot of a king-size bed, his arms folded across his chest.

She told him the police had just called her. "His mother is saying he was struggling with someone from the campaign."

"Was he?"

"No. I think it might be the FBI agent we identified at the Stein fundraiser. There's a surveillance tape. I've asked Bobby to get down to LAPD to review it. We'll know soon."

The left side of his face pulled down like he was having a stroke. "Shot by Mizz G. Damn, damn, damn."

"The White House will run full tilt with the story that someone from the campaign was pressuring him," Deirdre said.

"I'm so, so sorry."

Typical of him not to think of the politics.

She handed him the photo.

"I went to see him yesterday. Jake wanted you to have this."

Hansen glanced at it and then looked back at her, pain twisting his lips into a grimace.

"You went to see him? Why?"

"He told me at the Stein event that people from the government were pressuring him to tie you to the Oakland Four."

"His poor mother, she shot him?"

Before he got lost in his empathy, she said, "He wanted you to have the picture. He could have used it against you if he wanted."

Hansen studied the photo. His shoulders slumped. As if faint, he sat on the bed. Long muscular runner legs extended from boxer shorts.

"It was one of the few times I was with them. I thought it was cool that I was being cool. The dynamite was a stage prop."

Jesus, he talked as if they'd been going to a rock concert.

"They were trying to get Jake to implicate you, putting a lot of pressure on him."

"Who are they?"

"The White House, FBI, Justice, contractors, who knows? The same dirty crew as always."

"And his mother shot him?" he asked as if hoping he might not have heard correctly. "That's terrible."

When Hansen teared up, Deirdre did too. He hung his large head of curly brown hair like a bear in mourning. "I should have talked to him, not passed him off on you. I panicked. I think Jake was trying to patch things up between us." The sadness left his expression and was replaced by a narrow focus. "Let's find out who's behind this."

Deirdre sat beside him, took his hand, and put it on her thigh. "I'm not wearing any panties," she said.

He turned his head to her with narrowed eyes. "That's supposed to make me feel better?"

"Might for a while."

"A woman scorned. Sorry, I don't want to feel any worse."

"Well, I tried." She stood.

He reached for her hand. "You're really naked under there?"

"See for yourself." She turned to him as he ran his hand up her inner thigh. Seducing him was how she'd gotten him to trust her in the first place.

They forgot Jake Gillium for an hour.

Afterward, lying beside him, he tenderly held her. "You're not so tough," he said.

"I know. It's a shell. I'm a turtle. Touch me and I pull in my head."

"It's a beautiful head." He stroked her hair.

She liked his touch because it was genuine. She wanted him to be harder, but that wasn't who he was."

"You're not too bad yourself," she said.

He sighed. "Not such a great candidate these days. I'm not really made for this. Why did you pick me?"

"Because you were different. I saw something that voters saw. You're real."

"If you have any proof, I'm going to cry it from the rooftops."

She sighed. "We're working on it. Bobby Sutton thinks he knows the operative at the Stein party. We have a visual of his back as he left through Stein's private area. The guard at the door thinks he can make an ID if we show him a face."

"That's all? It could just be the other team. Spying on the other campaign is nothing new. Which is to say, you'd better get out of here."

She rolled over, spread her legs over his chest, and pinned him by the shoulders, using the strength she'd built up with weightlifting and martial arts. "You don't like me?"

He smiled. "Not enough to break up my marriage."

"I'll leave when I'm ready."

She wasn't surprised when he responded with renewed sexual energy. He had fantastic vigor and sexual prowess.

But he was right. She wasn't willing to lose the election to provide sexual ministry to her client. This would be the last time.

# SIX

## COPCOM

Blum hurried into the Joint Interagency Operations and Rapid Response Center in Norwalk, twelve miles from Gillium's store. He'd left his clothes in a dumpster and showed no visible evidence of being involved in a shooting an hour before. He had to keep it that way.

The Center had been established to respond quickly to terrorist situations by establishing more effective coordination, communication, and secure data sharing between law enforcement and security agencies.

Blum sat at the FBI station and entered his security clearance for the COPCOM system to gain access to the Los Angeles Police Department database. He found LAPD units were on the scene of a homicide at 1543 Laster Road. He quickly scanned the collected evidence, saw there was a surveillance video, and put a national security hold on the video. Classified top secret, the video would be difficult but not impossible to access. Next, he called a LAPD liaison and requested that LAPD units be removed and the investigation turned over to the FBI. It was going to be a long night.

━━━◉━━━

Willis Gradisky was described as a conservative columnist by the traditional press, or fake news, as the president liked to call the old print and television media. Gradisky was the publisher, editor, and reporter of

Poliscope.com, an online netzine whose importance was gauged by the eyes who read it—not the number of eyes but which eyes—how many of the gang of five hundred, the political and governmental elite who set the policy, chose and elected the candidates who ran the United States, who turned to Poliscope to read the latest gossip or inside information.

Gradisky attracted eyes and scooped fake news by getting up earlier, staying plugged in, digging deeper, digging faster, putting two and five together, and getting to seven before anyone else. Often stories came to him like stilettos thrust into the back of opponents in the wars of personal destruction.

Just before sunrise, an email from a trusted source arrived with a chime on his phone. Attached was the transcript of an LA police report. Thick highlighted lines marked where the statement of the suspect, Gertrude Gillium, had been highlighted.

S: *He was fighting with a man.*

I: *Did you recognize the man?*

S: *No. I don't think so.*

I: *Do you know anyone who your son might have had reason to fight with?*

S: *[crying] His father was killed not two feet from him. That's why I fired the gun. I was just trying to protect him.*

I: *I know this is painful, but I want to ask you some more questions.*

S: *[crying] My life is over. Over. I can't stand this. Nobody could. I shot my son. I can't answer any more questions now. I can't stand this.*

I: *I'm sorry to have to ask you these questions now, but we have to find the man your son was struggling with. Do you know of anyone who came to see him, called him, was anyone trying to get him to do anything?*

S: *[crying] Allan Hansen.*

I: *Allan Hansen?*

S: *The senator. Jake went to jail for him, took seven years of his life, his future for something Hansen did.*

I: *Do you think this man your son was struggling with was Allan Hansen?*

S: *No.*

*I: Then you didn't recognize him?*

*S: [crying] I can't talk anymore.*

The transcript was followed by a photo of a plastic bag holding a business card with a handwritten phone number on the back. An identifying tag read, *Physical evidence found on body of victim Jacob Gillium.*

A typed note at the bottom read, *"For background on Allan Hansen's involvement, see Oakland4.com."*

Gradisky pursed his lips. Was this an exclusive? How long did he have? He hurried to his basement office. His fingers flew to write and upload the story with a flash alert to the producers of fifty-six nationwide and local talk shows.

He studied the name on the business card and the telephone number. He should hold the number for himself if there was even the slimmest chance to get an exclusive interview with Owens before everyone else found her.

———◦———

After he'd tied down the Gillium crime scene, Blum was in Dalleck's office when he arrived at work at eight thirty in the morning.

The assistant US attorney's flaccid lips were pressed together with barely suppressed mirth. "Fox is saying that Gillium, the grocery store clerk you've been working on for the Hansen case, was shot last night by his own mother. Says he was fighting with someone Allan Hansen sent."

Blum couldn't match Dalleck's gleeful tone. "Anything about a video?"

"There is? Get it."

Blum felt the knot expanding in his throat.

"What's the progress on putting the squeeze on the other one, the West Virginia operation?" Dalleck asked.

"That's what I want to talk to you about." Blum hesitated. He had to make Dalleck think pulling the federal agents back was his idea. "What do you think we should do?"

Dalleck gave him an arrogant, scornful look. "Get up there and squeeze her titties until she goes public. Tell her what happened to her coconspirator could happen to her unless she comes clean."

"That's a great idea," Blum tried to put enthusiasm into his voice. "Strike while the iron is hot."

"Exactly."

"If we could only do it off book. There are too many eyes watching this case now, I mean, it's on Fox," he said as if they might reveal that the FBI was acting illegally to interfere with a federal election.

"I don't see that as being a problem," Dalleck said.

"It's just that we do have certain constraints," Blum said hesitantly.

Dalleck frowned as the realization sunk in that official acts by the US government to intimidate Lauren Bastini might become public knowledge.

Blum cast the line. "We need to go after her hard now, and I was hoping that you could think of some way we could really put the screws to her without leaving official fingerprints."

"You think that could be a problem, hmm?"

"We need your guidance on this."

"OK, I see your point. I don't want the AG to have to answer uncomfortable questions. Think we should have private contractors work on Bastini."

"Great idea. Good plan."

---

Deirdre was riding in the passenger seat of a staff car on the way to join Hansen for a meeting with the editorial board of the *Sacramento Bee*. With the phone pressed to her ear, she listened to a message from a number she didn't recognize.

The voice was friendly, young sounding, maybe a friend or classmate whose voice she'd forgotten. "Deirdre just wanted to call and say how terrible that was about Jake last night. Man o' man, they're gonna put your name all over the news. Give me a call, this is Willis Gradisky from Poliscope. Let's hear what you have to say. Give me a call."

She frowned. Was it possible to play into his hands and spin the story the other direction? No, not in his yard, maybe on a neutral turf, if any such thing still existed in today's news silos.

Her phone rang. It was Upton.

"You listening to the radio?" he asked.

She had to give it to him; he stayed informed.

"No."

"You've been doxed."

The term was new–a creation of the internet age–to reveal personal information about someone.

"You're on the LAPD transcript, name, and number. They practically have you pulling the trigger. You got anything solid we can throw back at them?"

"There's a tape. Bobby Hutton is trying to get it."

"How's the senator?"

"Light as a feather. I'm here to prevent him from personally going to console Mizz G. The whole business stinks. I feel like going with him."

"You wouldn't. Keep him off the subject."

She hung up on him. She was used to being behind the candidate, not in front.

———◆———

The meeting with the editorial board had gone well, Deirdre thought, nothing about the Oakland Four. During a discussion about a farm support bill, Hansen had reminded the three men and two women seated around the conference table that he'd grown up on a farm in the Central Valley. They'd laughed politely when he'd used an old joke that his family herded almonds.

Larry Grogan, the editor of the state affairs bureau, looked at a computer table set in front of his legal pad.

"Any other questions," Corinth, the editor in chief, looked around the table.

Grogan, tall with stooped shoulders, had a friendly, unassuming manner. "Just one more. Senator, are you concerned at all that in the coming election more will be made of your involvement with radical politics at Berkeley than in the past election?"

Hansen smiled and placed his hands flat on the table before him. "Good question, Larry. I fully expect terrorism and domestic security to be as large an issue as it was when I campaigned six years ago. I answered the charge then. It's a legitimate concern."

Grogan and the rest showed no response to his short reply.

Grogan raised his head from his sloping posture. "Have you had any recent contact with any of the people you were involved with in college, the so-called Oakland Four?"

*Here it comes*, Deirdre thought. She leaned forward from where she was seated against a wall. A flush rose up her neck. If the mainstream press were going to follow this story, he'd better get the right spin on it.

Hansen's eyes narrowed. "I knew all kinds of people in college but wasn't what you might call involved with any particular group. I fitted into lots of groups . . . just like I want to do now." He grinned.

Grogan tried to pry open the issue. "There have been persistent rumors that in college, you were actively involved with an environmental radical group that planned and attempted acts of sabotage."

Hansen's voice rose to a more forceful denunciation. "That's ridiculous. I was hardly a radical. I was a farm boy from Modesto who was placed in a freshman dorm room with a guy who got mixed up with the wrong crowd. I provided some testimony at his trial. That was the beginning and end of it."

"Would that be," Grogan glanced at the small screen, "Jacob Gillium?"

Hansen stared at the editor. "Yes."

Grogan's head sank again. "Do you have any comment on his death?"

Hansen looked up and didn't try to hide the sorrow in his eyes or voice. "I am, of course, greatly saddened by this terrible news. Jake Gillium turned his life around. He was an active and important community leader."

The editorial board observed him as if judging how sad he was.

Deirdre thought it would have been a better strategy for Hansen to act as if he was learning of the death for the first time. But the senator lacked the guile for that.

Grogan looked down, past Hansen, at her, then back at Hansen.

Deirdre tensed, sensing a springing trap, maybe what a rat feels as the bar drops on its neck.

"We have information that the police found your campaign manager's name on Jake Gillium's body. His mother is saying that when her son was shot, he was struggling with someone from your campaign. Any comment?"

Hansen looked unflinchingly at the editor. "No, only my deep sorrow to hear about this tragedy."

Hansen could obfuscate when he wanted.

Grogan rose to a near-upright position and focused beyond the table at Deirdre. "You're Deirdre Owens, the senator's campaign manager." He introduced her like qualifying a witness. "Were you interviewed by the police?"

Deirdre's eyes narrowed as if she might slap the man. "Why are you asking me? Has someone told you?"

Grogan twisted his lips and backed off.

"No doubt the opposition is seeking every opportunity to take advantage of this tragedy," she said.

Hansen stood. "Sorry, guys, I have to get going."

Deirdre stepped to his side.

Corinth, gray-haired with sun flush on his cheeks, came around the table and shook Hansen's hand. "Thank you very much, Senator, for spending this time with us. I'm sure it has helped us to understand your positions much more clearly. And Deirdre, we understand someone is trying to tie you to this tragedy. It's unlikely that we are the only ones with this information."

"Thanks for the tip," she said with too much scorn.

Hansen hesitated and said, "I may have testified against Jake, but I never thought he was directly involved. He made a youthful mistake and paid a dear price. Now . . ."

He was losing control. Deirdre resisted the urge to take him by the hand.

"He paid the ultimate price. I'm going to do everything in my power to get to the bottom of this terrible, terrible tragedy. Jake was no terrorist."

Corinth nodded and quickly patted him on the back as if to comfort him.

The other editors watched him. No one was smiling.

Grogan, taller by three inches than Hansen, was so hunched that his head hung down at Hansen's eye level. "Sorry about that," he apologized. "Maybe we can help set the facts straight."

Hansen breathed deeply and said in a firm tone, "Jake Gillium was a strong voice for his community. He should be remembered for that."

"Check who's pushing the story," she said to Grogan. "And you'll find who Jake was struggling with."

"Do you have any information on that?" the editor asked.

"We're working on it," Hansen said quickly before she might say something about an FBI agent.

She followed him and his entourage to a white SUV and sat in the front passenger seat.

This was war. The newspaper hacks knew they were being manipulated. No doubt they weren't the only ones. Hansen had to respond, use their own media to demand the security tape be released, to prove that FBI Agent George Blum was the one struggling with Gillium.

As she was driven down 21st heading to the 80, she tuned the radio to one of the many stations broadcasting Rick Rage live. Know your enemy. She didn't have to wait long to hear.

"They would like us to think," Rick Rage's mellifluent voice flowed out of the speakers, "that character doesn't count. We're here to tell them, yes, it does. Character does count. Take, for instance, Senator Allan Hansen from the People's Republic of Berkeley. It is common knowledge that he was a pot-smoking Berkeley radical. OK, fine. Let him come out and admit it. I would have much greater respect for him if he did than trying to act like he just happened to be there when his old lady, Lauren Bastini, planned to blow up a laboratory conducting research on producing the seeds we need to feed the planet. Oh, I know, you say . . ."

He changed his voice and began speaking with a lisp. "Rick, he testified against Bastini and his best friend, doesn't that prove he's innocent?"

"No!" Rage shouted. "It doesn't! You can't fool us, Comrade Hansen. We know what you did. Come out and admit it. And let the people of California decide if they want a terrorist representing them in the US Senate. You might be surprised, Comrade. After all, it is the land of fruits and nuts. You might be surprised at how many people out there would think having a terrorist in the Senate is just fine. We've got Nancy on the line. What do you think?"

"Hi, Jake. Major rage from Loma Linda."

"Major rage to you, Nancy. What enlightenment and inciting insights from the pinnacle of preciosity may I provide you with this morning?"

Nancy had a sweet voice like a housewife who had stopped cleaning the kitchen floor long enough to call Rage. "I was just listening to you about our soon-to-be former senator, Allan Hansen. I understand he's the one stopping the Senate from bringing up the Sentinel Act for a vote."

"Of course he is! Of course, he wants to weaken our ability to fight terrorism. A leopard doesn't change his spots. Once a liberal, always a liberal, or in this case, a terrorist. We'll be right back. Stay tuned!"

She must have missed being called out by name. There was no doubt that Deirdre Owens would be on every talking point of every news show controlled by the opposition.

Fight fire with fire. If the opposition was going to use leaks, she had her own venues to shape the story of the death of Jake Gillium.

# SEVEN

## THE GRAY ANARCHIST

Her back stiffened was as hard as the varnished planks of the desk on which she planted her fist as she read the website permanentecorevolution.org, the website Jake Gillium had founded to fight environmental destruction.

Jake Gillium is the latest martyr in the US government's war on its own people. Gillium was murdered while defending his mother and their family store.

Sources say that Jake Gillium was struggling with an FBI agent . . .

Lauren Bastini couldn't read more. Jake must have called her hours before he was murdered to say that the FBI was pressuring him to come out publicly against Allan Hansen.

She had received an email from Special Agent George Blum.

*The FBI has determined that you possess information relevant to an ongoing investigation into prior criminal activity by Allan Hansen. Your cooperation is necessary for national security reasons. Please immediately call me to discuss this matter.*

The bastard had left his personal number.

Thirty-six years and the FBI was still harassing her.

A mixture of sweetness for all nature and distrust of her fellow species and their work, sarcastic about people who offended her, and vengeful of those who harmed her, Bastini had only asked to be left alone.

Personal injustices and environmental degradation fueled a passion for revenge. Hot rage furrowed her brows. The grim line of her mouth warned she was ready to act.

Gray hair, self-cut without the aid of a mirror, rested like a feral fern above swollen eyes, missing eyebrows, and lashes that would never grow again. Fit for a seventy-three-year-old woman, her chest was as flat as a man's. She hadn't bothered with prosthetics when cancer took her tits. The fowl, goats, dogs, cats, and bees that shared her West Virginia plot didn't mind her carved-up chest any more than they did the hypertrophic burn scars that spread like purple branches of pain up her neck and across her face, remnants from the firefight at the Monsanto biotech research facility.

The ducks at the pond at the bottom of the hill started to quack, alerting the penned dogs who barked their warnings.

Through double-pane glass framed by rough-hewn logs, she saw a car parked on the road at the foot of the steep slope that led up to the house. They didn't look like honey buyers. Two men in suits were opening the metal gate that hung across the dirt driveway despite the no trespassing sign.

The war she'd been preparing for had arrived.

She went to a closet, took out a T3x sniper rifle, and stuffed a Glock .45 auto into the front pouch of her denim overalls. She set an AR-15, the civilian version of the M16, and a green combat bag filled with ammunition and grenades on the floor, ready for use.

The men had disappeared behind a bend in the road. She bent on her front porch and rested the gun barrel on the split-log railing, sighting through the scope left of a hickory tree where they would emerge.

She closed her eyes and breathed deeply. Killing these would bring too much heat too quickly. She had a bigger plan.

She picked up the AR-15 and combat bag. Out the kitchen windows, she didn't see anyone approaching from the forest or the clearing in which white boxes containing her beehives rested.

She opened the basement door and locked it behind her. A single light bulb hanging from a cord revealed a bearded man dressed in a long white kameez and baggy pants. Behind him, his wife dressed in a hijab, a white scarf folded around her head and under her chin, huddled in a darkened corner with three children.

"Know how to use this, Shaquat?" Bastini asked as she descended the wooden stairs, holding out the AR-15.

The man's puffy eyes expanded with alarm. "Please, Miss, the children . . ."

His wife whispered urgently to him in Punjabi.

"Keep them quiet," Bastini said and moved to the side of the stairs, seeking an angle that would give her a good shot at anyone who tried to come through the door.

Above, she could hear knocking on the front door, then the sounds of shuffling feet over their heads. Someone came to the basement door.

Bastini crouched. The refugee family cowered together in fear.

The door above them rattled.

Bastini's hand tightened around the stock of the rifle. The burn scars on her face and neck throbbed.

The door held against the pressure on the other side. A man's voice said, "It's locked."

Bastini waited for an hour, listening to the silence. She wasn't raised to be locked in a cellar with Pakistani refugees. She came from privilege, private schools, and academic achievement.

Her mother, who'd dressed her like an expensive doll so nobody would doubt that they were rich, had married up to be the wife of an entitled and weak country club golfer. The family didn't deserve the wealth from a vacuum cleaning business sold door to door by impoverished salesmen during the Depression. Lauren belonged on the shores of the Chesapeake Bay with her mother's father, Papa Dave, raking the shallows for oysters.

She'd last seen her parents in Riverside, California, a few weeks before the bombing. She'd been skinny and dressed in old jeans and a T-shirt. She could have made her mother happy by letting her buy her new clothes, but she hadn't. She'd felt weak for eating the abundance of factory-raised food.

Jimmy, her true love, her inspiration, quoting William Blake that free love was universal liberty. She'd dallied with Jake, the virgin Allan Hansen, and many others as casually as asking their name.

Now, scarred and old, she'd dream of Jimmy and her as they were when still young, filled with passion for each other and environmental justice. She'd awaken and wonder why she hadn't died with him.

The time had come to slaughter the wicked, start the revolution, wage war on those who violated nature, and do what she was supposed to with what was left of her life.

Upstairs, the boxes and jars of honey ready for shipping had been moved around. Her eyes searched the dark corners of the ceiling and bookcase. She wondered where they had put the cameras and microphones.

She threw open the wooden doors of a root cellar behind the kitchen and pulled out a heavy nylon tote bag filled with weapons. The eighty-pound bag strained her back as she loaded her arsenal into the rear of her black Jeep.

Shaquat crept after her.

"I'd clear out of here if I was you," Bastini said to the Pakistani as she opened the car door.

"May I ask where you are going, ma'am?"

Bastini climbed in, looked out the side window at him, and muttered, "To war."

She stopped at a bend. When nothing came up the road after her, she figured they'd put a tracker on her car.

Her mountain hideaway would be the place to make her last stand, but she had too much to do before that final redoubt.

She drove slowly past the brick buildings of Lewisburg. When she reached I-66 and crossed the Greenbrier River, she decided amateurs were following her. The feds would have arrested her as soon as she revealed her weapons stash. Thirty years of harassment had taught her as much about their tactics as a field agent would know.

On the Washington Beltway, she exited onto Cabin John Road, stopped, and waited while several cars followed her up the off ramp. When she saw the burgundy SUV with the two suits, she pulled onto the highway in the opposite direction. The Bronco turned and followed her. She changed direction again. When she passed the car, she recognized the blond man driving. He had been one of the two who had come to the cabin.

Once they were out of sight, she turned on a cell jammer to block the signal of the bug they'd placed on her car, waited until their vehicle drove by, pulled out behind them, and the hunted became the hunter.

A better tracker than they were, she stayed several cars behind but was able to follow them down the George Washington Parkway to a town house near Union Station.

She circled the block and focused reflector binoculars on the front of the narrow brick building. A brass plaque read *Domestic Security Association*.

Who or what the fuck were the Domestic Security Association? Whoever they were, they'd picked the wrong person to fuck with.

As she drove away, her heart began to beat normally, and the tenseness in her muscles eased. Her adrenal levels were at the lowest since she'd left her place.

She'd miss her life as a beekeeper. Weaver Knob was a sanctuary, and she could believe the beast had forgotten her. The persecution was over. The ravenous, bloodthirsty tyrant whose burning claw had scarred her face and put her in Tehachapi prison had reached out for her again.

Well, they'd found her, and she had a better idea of what to do. She needed to go underground for a few days and prepare. But she wasn't going to hide for long. She wanted to make her statement, to use her life as an instrument of resistance as her Muslim brothers were doing every day.

She needed to marshal her resources. Three decades of collecting weapons had given her a nice armory hidden in an abandoned mine near Morris Creek up the Seneca Trail. The bags she'd carried from the farm had been chosen for defense.

She needed her offensive weapons, more firepower than any of the radicals from the sixties ever had. The Weather Underground, Symbionese Liberation Army, and Black Panthers had never had the weapons the Second Amendment crowd had assured every American they could buy with minimal government interference.

But she had more than that. She decided she'd start her campaign with the Russian RPG-7 Kahlid Shaifqueur had given her for hiding his cousin's family.

As she drove across Capitol Hill with all its supposed security, her eyes moved to the Capitol dome. The marble bell of the Capitol dome looked as fragile as confectionery sugar. The city of symbolic American pride seemed less defensible than a backyard tree fort. Targets were everywhere and plentiful.

Now she was committed to action. She wanted to do it right. Use the same meticulous planning that Al Qaeda did. She wanted to make a statement with clarity. Simple, so that people who mattered in this country, the ones who were so often forgotten in these government buildings, would understand. She wanted them to know that she loved this country, loved liberty and justice, and what the US was supposed to stand for before the oppressors had conquered it.

She had to know more about her enemy. Who was the Domestic Security Association? The men who had followed her were stupid and careless, but they would report what they had observed to their bosses, and the alert would be out. The US police state would have all its million eyes and ears looking for her.

She parked in front of the Martin Luther King Library on Ninth Street. The glass-and-steel office building had none of the fake Greek and Roman pomp of federal buildings. She joined tourists and street people using the free internet connection in the lobby and searched "Domestic Security Association."

What she read caused her to frown. Had she panicked unnecessarily and been flushed out of her home by a bunch of right-wing lobbyists?

No, this was an example of more government outsourcing. The FBI, CIA, and Pentagon were like other American businesses, just trying to hide what was on their books.

One piece on the DSA web page caught her attention.

*Be sure to make your plans early for the DSA annual Winter Conference to be held this year at the beautiful Mission Inn in Riverside, California.*

Bastini smiled. She might have to make plans to attend their conference.

Next, she searched for "Allan Hansen" and found the Poliscope piece that identified Deirdre Owens. Another Poliscope article attacked him for not having his own house in California and gave an address in Redlands where he lived with his brother. She didn't mind that. So what if he wasn't rich enough to afford a house in California?

She imagined him as she'd known him as an impressionable freshman at Cal. He and Jake had been as soft and pliable as dough. She'd taken Allan Hansen to her bed because he was cute, a muscular farm boy. Jake, soft and Jewish, had the better intellect, but who fucked a more brilliant mind?

She wrote down his brother's address. Plenty of targets. The war had begun. The new American revolution was about to commence.

# EIGHT

## AMERI BATTLESTONE

Deirdre walked up the driveway she shared with Ameri Battlestone, a lawyer, a published author on radical Black politics, and her landlord. He'd done very well collecting attorney fees paid by the Civil Rights Act violators and rented her a granny flat on his property in San Mateo.

"Deirdre." Battlestone smiled. "Come in."

"Are you alone?" She stepped through his front door.

"Yeah, Saturday night, and I ain't got nobody," Sam Cooke's voice rang from him.

She followed him through his living room. He had the height and solid build of the wide receiver he'd been on the Stanford football team. Handsome with a broad smile that enhanced even, white teeth, his voice rose from deep within his chest in a baritone he used well as a singer. Beside a fireplace stood a three-foot-high box that looked like a cross between an amplifier and a sound system. A microphone and sturdy professional music stand held a thick three-ring binder, evidence of his passion for karaoke.

She'd gone with him to a gathering of serious practitioners of singing along with the music to popular songs. These were not the giggling imitators stumbling over words in bars and street festivals. Mostly Japanese and Koreans, they had put on startling performances, but none as powerful as Battlestone.

She'd been amazed at his transformation in the softly lit Oakland bar, marveling that anyone could do this that well. Wearing an electric-blue tuxedo worthy of a Las Vegas lounge, he'd held the microphone in a professional light grip, leaned back, and closed his eyes as the strings and piano introduced the melody to a classic tune.

*A song of love surrounds me*
*Oh, the things you do to me*
*Never has anyone meant more to me . . .*

"Back so soon?" Battlestone's voice filled the house. Miles Davis's *Kind of Blue* played from small speakers set on a built-in floor-to-ceiling bookcase.

"It's been crazy."

"Last I heard, you were the subject of a right-wing bête noire. Ho, ho, ho." Battlestone's eyes gleamed. "I was just decanting a Shiraz. He led her into his kitchen and poured the deep plum-colored wine into two sparkling glasses. "So, tell."

She fingered the stem of the wineglass. Her grandmother's aquamarine ring glinted on the long slender finger of her right hand. "I believe we're in the midst of something bigger than the Hansen campaign."

There is pleasure in good wine and story. They leaned against the quartz countertop. Battlestone's expression went from amusement to rapt attention, nodding his head, not interrupting her theory that the campaign was under assault by the White House.

Battlestone picked up the bottle and ushered her into the living room. They sat in overstuffed chairs before a cherry wood coffee table. Battlestone crossed his legs and leaned back.

One of the many things she appreciated about him was the way he listened. His eyes were somewhat lowered, and he rocked his head. He was thinking, turning the facts around, looking at them from many sides, and distilling the core issues.

She leaned back in the chair and held the glass perched on the armrest.

Battlestone shifted in his seat. "You fear the ideal of impartiality of our police services in general elections is tested once again."

He was pleading before a jury. His tone of voice became more oratorical, his enunciation more distinct. His eyes narrowed in consternation. "When the military or police use their power to influence elections, we veer to tyranny. This was one of the great fears of the founders, one that they hoped the separation of powers would thwart. I smell an old and familiar scent around this, a hoary hand reaching from the past."

If he'd been telling a ghost story around a campfire, he couldn't have sounded more ominous.

"COINTELPRO, FBI counterintelligence. One would expect them to be released from their crypt. They were beaten back and contained after the abuses of Nixon, but I'm not surprised to see this rogue unleashed again by the fearful in our society."

He leaned forward in his seat. She'd rarely seen him so passionate. "And how are we to know? In the seventies, we had an active, independent press that demanded access to our leaders. Now the fourth estate is led around, sequestered, embedded, and shamelessly manipulated. Its ranks are infiltrated with political operatives who make no secret of their bias and go back and forth between reporting and serving their political masters with impunity."

She nodded as he confirmed her fears.

"The Congress as it sits today is in shambles. The people have responded to the abuses of the past, but will their courage last? The culture of fear sits heavily on Democrats' breasts, as it does on Republicans. The judiciary is so ridden with conformists parading as conservatives that it's getting harder and harder to find an independent mind in that branch." He looked at her with an intense gaze. "Would you like me to assist you?"

She pushed back her hair. "Thanks, that's why I wanted to talk to you in person. I've been very public with my suspicions, my accusations."

"And right you are. I'm honored that you would ask me to help defend the integrity of the American political process." Battlestone raised his hand as if to show her something in his palm. "Not all in government are eager to see the collapse of the separation of powers. I suspect a few of my well-placed friends will be more than ready to assist us to battle the dragons of oligarchy. We are talking about bullies—little different from the schoolyard. The way to treat them is to stand up to them, or they will continue to torment and grow bolder in their sadism. Implore our senator to raise the alarm and use this as an example of how we have gone too far down a dangerous path. Call back the evil COINTELPRO before they can do any more damage and grow any stronger."

Deirdre studied him. He certainly had a flair for metaphors—hoary hands rising from crypts, dragons, schoolyard bullies, sadists—but did she want him messing in her campaign? Upton had a point. The more they talked about FBI interference, the more attention they called to Hansen's involvement with the Oakland Four.

"The senator wants proof. He can't be seen tilting at windmills. He's already fighting against an image of being a radical."

Battlestone sat, acting more relaxed as if he had decided on his course. "There are extraordinary times when citizens must rise up and defend our rights, or we will lose them."

Deirdre nodded and took a sip of her wine. Hansen would like that attitude. Maybe she should get them together, but the campaign tactician in her wanted to keep Hansen clear of a public fight with the FBI. Let Ameri's friends call the alarm.

Battlestone appeared to understand. He said softly, "Trust me, Deirdre. I believe I can pull this off while protecting your client's confidentiality."

"Be careful. I've gotten too far in front of this. If we are right, we've alerted them, and they will be coming after us. They've placed a national security restriction on the store security video. It'll take a court order to see it."

———◦———

Dressed in a dress shirt tailored to his muscular frame, Battlestone sat before a computer monitor in his office.

The Oakland Four. Things have a way of coming around. He remembered his professor, Angela Parkston, talking about the case as part of her Race, Politics, and Culture course. She'd worn Maasai olokesena skirts, blouses, and head wraps, lecturing the mostly Black Stanford undergrads, many of them athletes like him. "Them going after these white kids diverted attention from the right-wing racial terrorists. Showed they were fair." She'd dragged out the last word.

He expanded his search through national legal and journalistic records. By ten o'clock in the morning, he had a good idea that Angela Parkston was pretty much right. The so-called Oakland Four was a bunch of Berkeley environmental activists who had been easily infiltrated, set up, and killed or severely injured—hardly a national organization, but then neither was Timothy McVeigh, the white boy who'd blown up the federal building in Tulsa. An attitude that *they were trying to save the Earth* didn't fly then, and it surely wouldn't today. If Allan Hansen were tied directly to them, he would certainly lose his reelection bid.

Battlestone's search produced the Poliscope piece and articles in organs of the opposite persuasion—on the right accusing Hansen, on the left the FBI. The sum of two risked what worried Deirdre—the story going viral and calling attention to Hansen's alleged terrorist past.

The Los Angeles Police Department could have leaked the police interview with Mrs. Gillium. There were plenty in the constabulary who would want to hurt Allan Hansen by providing the police transcript to the press.

This was going to take some delicate handling.

He called one of his *ladies*.

He'd met District Court Judge June Wallace when she'd come to Stanford for post-doctoral work. She'd turned to him when her marriage to a former basketball star had broken up. They shared a notion that one day there would be more for them than sincere friendship.

"Lady June Bug." He drawled her name in his best Lou Rawls voice.

"Why you calling me? One of your women left you?"

They spoke in a purposeful anti-sophisticate Black parlance. Anyone eavesdropping on them might assume from their accents that they were listening to the conversation of two Southern neighbors, not two fine legal minds.

"No, baby. I got something else on my mind this fine morning. Something I've talked to you about before."

"What's that?"

"These people who would kill our country to save it."

"What they done now?"

"I'm not right sure about that yet. That's why I'm calling you. Appears somebody released a police report that mentions Allan Hansen."

When he told her the story, Judge Wallace was not impressed.

"So, somebody got excited down at the police station and faxed a copy of a report to somebody. That's hardly a conspiracy."

"I got a feeling about this. It's what I've been talking to you about. You remember what the FBI was doing in the sixties and early seventies. I think they're coming back with a vengeance. Allan Hansen is one of our strongest protectors of civil liberties. He's blocking the Senate from passing the Sentinel Act. This is their way of putting pressure on him."

"Honey, you know how many intelligence agencies there are out there now? I had an eavesdropping case with stipulations of twelve hundred government organizations and more than nineteen hundred private companies working on counterterrorism, homeland security, and intelligence in some ten thousand locations across the United States. And that's not even counting state and local law enforcement agencies."

"We still got to resist. Messing with elections, locking up people they don't like . . . And when they have everything under their control, how are we ever going to stop them?"

"Ameri, Ameri, my Paul Revere. Baby, what do you want me to do about it? The man's a United States senator. Can't he find out what he needs to know?"

"Apparently they've put a national security tag on a key piece of evidence."

"There may be an invasion-of-privacy issue, and I'm sure LAPD doesn't want their investigations published, but if it's classified, that's a hard nut to crack without serious national security implications."

"June, I think this is something more than police station gossip. We're not talking about a First Amendment press issue. We're talking about a dedicated effort by the FBI to intervene in the political process."

"Well, that would be singing the president's tune. Do you think the White House is involved?"

"Could very well be. You know, I wouldn't be calling you unless I thought this was something bigger than a political smear. Think about it. They've got all these new tools to spy on whatever you're doing, saying, or holding. Now they want to pass the Sentinel Act to expand eavesdropping and limit probable cause for search and seizure. We're not that far from losing it all. I personally don't want to give my freedom back."

The judge was silent. Battlestone did not say anything more, letting his words settle.

Wallace sighed. "Let me see what I can find out. Email me what you got."

"On the way. Now, what did you do last night?"

<hr />

Judge Wallace was one of twenty-eight federal judges conducting trials in the United States district court for the Central District of California. Born into an upper-class family with a lawyer father and a corporate executive mother, she had gone to Howard over the Ivies that had admitted her. She maintained what some called her "Blackness" with pride, able to move between different social strata and lingua with ease and comfort. To keep from being swallowed by her judicial robe, she always wore a colorful blouse with a wide collar or scarf tied around her neck. She was sitting atop the raised dais Thursday morning, listening to a diversity argument between two software vendors, when Assistant US Attorney Anthony Belligoni entered the courtroom.

Wallace gently tapped her gavel and announced a half-hour recess.

Within her chambers was a spacious wood-paneled office. By the time Wallace had reached the bench, everything was on the way to being computerized. A library of books, what her very Yale, very Brentwood predecessor would have spent an hour climbing around his shelves to find, could be searched on her computer in seconds.

Wallace had kept some of the old volumes to make her office look like those depicted in film and television. Also, they had beauty with their finely woven covers and stately patched titles. But she had given the majority of the shelf space to a collection of African Caribbean, African Brazilian, and African American art.

She didn't bother taking off her robe and was listening to messages behind her desk when Belligoni entered.

He was thickly built with curly black hair and expressive lips that curled when he was angry or spread in a wide smile when pleased.

"Sit down, Tony." Wallace pointed to one of two chairs before her desk. She scribbled a note, set the phone down, and leaned toward the man. "I'm concerned about something, Tony."

He crossed his legs and smoothed the expensive merino cloth of his trouser leg. "What's that, Judge?"

They had first worked together on a case involving the LAPD Rampart Division.

"I hear an LAPD police report about Allan Hansen was leaked into the media. The testimony had barely been taken down when it was on the internet. What I'm concerned about is somebody in the police department messing around in a political race."

"Wouldn't be the first time. What did the report say?"

"It was that case over in Boyle Heights where the mother shot her son."

Belligoni pursed his lips. "Yeah, I read about that. Trying to tie it to the feds."

"Some say it was Hansen. Here." Wallace tossed a printout of Poliscope to him.

Belligoni read it quickly and looked up.

"Rick Rage was talking about it," Wallace said.

Belligoni gave a crooked grin. "You listen to Rick Rage?"

The judge acted as if there was nothing humorous in Belligoni's jest, maintaining her serious air. "When it suits my purpose. Somebody is using a witness statement to attack an elected official. I want to know who."

Belligoni grimaced. "That might be difficult. You know how hard it is to find a leaker."

The judge scrunched up her face in doubt. "There must be some way the police are protecting their evidence. If you put it out there for everyone to see, how are you all ever going to use it in court?"

Belligoni showed his teeth with a crooked grin. "Good question."

The judge scowled. "I don't like unwarranted dissemination of private information. It's too easy to tamper with and raises chain-of-custody issues. I haven't seen much of it in my court yet, but I tell you this, Tony." She leaned forward and pointed her thin finger at the large man. "I wouldn't hesitate to suppress evidence that's been broadcast around the world if I thought it had been tainted."

He opened his hands. "Local law enforcement is our eyes and ears. They have to be in the intelligence loop. We've made some cross-references that we would never have caught in the past."

Wallace pressed her hands together in a position of prayer and leaned across the desk. "I know, but my concerns have to do with access. How secure is this data? How do we know that someone isn't tampering with evidence?"

Belligoni looked at his knees while gathering his thoughts, then challenged the judge's argument. "We know who has access to the data."

Wallace's intense black eyes narrowed into a piercing focus. "I'm going to schedule a hearing on this in camera Monday morning. I want you to come back and tell me what you find out about this case and what we're doing to keep the police out of elections."

Belligoni cleared his throat and shifted his weight before saying, "Look, I know this is an important issue . . ."

Wallace had already looked away from him and was entering the ten o'clock hearing into her docket.

———◆———

Monday morning, Belligoni again sat before Wallace's desk.

The petite woman was dressed in her black judicial robe, a wide chartreuse collar lying around her neck and over her shoulders.

Wallace sat back in the deep cavity of her chair. "What do you have, Tony?"

"The Gillium file has been sealed. I can't get at it." He shrugged. "But then neither can anyone from Los Angeles Police Department. That argues against them."

"And points to the feds. How many people had access to the LAPD data files?" Wallace asked.

Belligoni shrugged. "A lot. Let me call in my only witness."

As Wallace watched him go to the door, she frowned. Judges weren't supposed to conduct their own investigations. They were to run the trial and make sure each side's rights were preserved and evidence properly introduced. Well, this wasn't her case, and if it ever came to her court, she would recuse herself.

———◆———

Detective Cork Johnson had gotten the call from his captain. Be at First Street at ten o'clock. Cork waited in the judge's reception area in a chair set against the wall. His second-best suit made him look credible, which is how a cop wants to look in court.

Never mind that it was his day off. Nobody had any idea what it was about, but you don't argue with a federal judge. He'd never been before Judge June Wallace before, but she was known as a liberal appointee, more likely to give a crook a break than other judges.

Cork looked at a woman working at a desk behind a counter. He'd been in court a hundred times but never anything like this. Could be a corruption probe, but that would be the grand jury, not a meeting with a judge in her chambers.

Cork pulled a folded white handkerchief out of his pocket and patted his forehead. Sweat created a bright sheen on his dark skin. Damn, why did they have to keep him waiting? It was like being called to the principal's office. A thousand things you'd done wrong kept you guessing about why you'd been caught. Maybe he should have gone to the Police Protective League and asked for legal counsel. No, better not to have jumped the gun. Wait and see what they want.

Finally, the door opened, and he was admitted to the chamber by Assistant US Attorney Belligoni. Cork thought that if this had been a television show, Belligoni would have been better cast as a Mafia enforcer.

"Sit down here, Officer." Belligoni pointed to a wooden chair at a conference table.

Cork lowered his big frame and filled up the seat. Belligoni sat across from him. The judge sat at the head of the table. Cork felt the dampness rising on his forehead, but he didn't pull out the handkerchief.

The judge was a little lady. But the way she looked right through him made his guts twitch. He must really be in some shit.

"Thank you for coming, Lieutenant Cork." Belligoni sounded like he was from New York.

"No problem." Cork's voice got higher the more nervous he was. His tone hadn't been this pitch since his wife caught him with his old girlfriend.

"This is Judge June Wallace."

"Your Honor." He nodded at her, and then looked away from her probing stare. She reminded him of his older sister, who still scared the crap out of him.

"We want to ask you about your homicide investigation at Gillium's grocery store," Belligoni said.

The tightness left his chest. At least he knew what he was dealing with.

"Can you tell us what happened?"

Cork's voice was back to its lower register. He figured the senator had heard from his aide that he was asking about him. Now he had a federal judge and a DA finding out why.

In his practiced court voice, trained not to draw any legal conclusions, he described the scene in factual detail, including the struggle between Jake Gillium and a man caught on the security camera.

"What happened to these video images?" Belligoni asked.

"The tape from the security camera was taken by crime scene technicians, following all . . ."

The judge impatiently interrupted. "Did you view the security tape?"

"Yes, ma'am. The crime scene investigators have a portable video player, which lets us quickly look at the evidence to see what we're looking for."

The judge pressed him like he had something to hide, her hands tightly clasped in front of her. "Did you see anything on these tapes that raised any issues of national security?"

Cork shrugged his big shoulders. "Not that I know of, but that's not my area."

Belligoni smiled. "Look, Detective, we're not trying to uncover any wrongdoing on your part."

The judge did not act so reassuringly. She leaned forward, looking like some kind of bat about to fly across the table at him. "Do you know how the LAPD transcript on this murder investigation was released to the press?"

Cork firmly said, "I doubt it was anyone from my department. FBI had this case under wraps before we got out the door."

The judge looked at him with narrowed eyes as if he was hiding something. "So, you think someone from the bureau released the transcript."

Cork shifted in his seat. Sweat again rose over his eyebrows. He sure as hell didn't want to get in the crossfire between the FBI and LAPD. "I can't say for sure, Your Honor."

"The feds aren't the only ones who have access to that evidence," Belligoni said.

Cork was unused to this kind of give and take in a courtroom. His eyes moved from the judge to Belligoni and back to the judge.

"But you said you can't get into it," the judge countered.

"Not at that level," Belligoni admitted.

The judge glared at Cork. "Was there anything about the crime scene or your conversation that led you to believe that Senator Hansen was involved in the homicide?"

"Yes, ma'am. We found a name in the victim's pocket. I don't recall what it was."

"Deirdre Owens?" Wallace pressed.

"Yes, ma'am, that sounds right."

"The name was released to the press. That's how I know," Wallace said.

"We turned over all the evidence to the FBI."

"Is that a common practice?" Wallace asked.

"When it's federal jurisdiction."

"Was it?"

"No, ma'am. Not that I could see, but I didn't explore the matter once we dropped out of the investigation." He squeezed his large hands together on the table in an unconscious imitation of the judge. "I mean, if I was conducting the investigation, I'd want to see who the man was on the videotape that was struggling with the victim when he was shot by Mrs. Gillium. If he was from the senator's office then maybe there is some connection to Senator Hansen . . ." Realizing he'd gone too far, he hastened to conclude, ". . . but it's in the bureau's hands now."

Cork was on his feet the second they let him go. He hunched his shoulders and thrust his head out as he strode down the hall of the courthouse, trying to figure out how he could get out of this shit. Hansen must be plenty worried to put this much heat on him. Damn, he hated politics.

Judge Wallace waited until the door had shut behind Johnson before saying to Belligoni, "Laws have been broken, Tony. There is more than enough probable cause to bring this before the grand jury. If that file is classified, then someone leaked classified information. Also, it's a violation to access LAPD evidence for anything but police businesses. I want you to bring this before the grand jury."

Belligoni did not respond right away. He crossed his legs and smiled his crooked grin. "I don't know, Judge, if it's misuse by an agent or department, we can take care of it from the inside and avoid all the national security implications of a public airing of the anti-terrorism aspects of the system. If you are talking about challenging the counterintelligence system, I can guarantee resistance from Washington. They will argue national security, and we'll have a tough row to hoe to get anywhere."

Wallace scoffed. "Look, it's one or the other. Either it's classified and sensitive, and someone leaked classified information, or it's not classified, and there should be no problem in identifying who was struggling with Gillium when he was shot. Why are they suppressing that? Why can't we view that same information?"

His smile was nearly a frown. "Depends on how high it goes. Those at the top might not leave a trace."

"You think it goes that high?"

His eyes seemed more hooded and sadder than unusual. "I wouldn't be surprised." He slapped his hands on his upper thigh and stood. "But we'll have to see. Maybe it's just an LA cop listening to too much Rick Rage. We'll see."

After Belligoni left, the judge had five minutes until she was due back on the bench. She walked past the twelve-foot-high walnut bookcases lining her chambers. A green-and-red Haitian *drapeau* voodoo flag appeared to be the focus of her stare, but it was not the kissing snakes on the satin background that held her attention. She was deep in thought. Federal judges were supposed to be independent and appointed for life, but there were a lot of ways you could get in trouble as a judge. Chief judges and judicial councils could make your life miserable with the cases you were assigned or weren't assigned, examining your rulings. She might even be subject to impeachment if she jeopardized national security, or at least be passed over for higher benches.

The Supreme Court had so far upheld the constitutional rights of courts to limit unwarranted searches and seizures by the government based on national security. If Belligoni was right and there was a genuine national security issue, what could she do? Politicians complained about judicial activism, interpreting the law in a way that changed the law. A judge was a judge. If she started collecting evidence and issuing subpoenas to federal officials, she would be violating the same separation of powers she was trying to protect. She had to respect the Constitution even if she was trying to save it. She needed a grand jury investigation.

Could she count on Belligoni to develop the evidence? He'd been quite aggressive in the Rampart investigation, but there they'd been uncovering outright criminal activity by the police. His boss, US Attorney Hillary Morgenstern, was appointed by the president. Belligoni could and would be fired if he displeased her.

Releasing a transcript involving an elected official was probably against the rules and procedures but hardly amounted to a crime, nothing like dealing in drugs and contract murders. It was one thing to expose a rogue agent or division and quite another to take on the FBI and national security apparatus. What she was asking him to investigate was the manipulation of law enforcement activities by some very powerful members of the federal government, perfectly capable of squashing underlings like Anthony Belligoni and ruining his career.

This was the kind of thing that Congress should investigate, but she agreed with Battlestone that the judiciary should also be involved. Sometimes it took both other branches of government to balance the third. But could Belligoni build a good enough case to convince sixteen average citizens that their government was interfering with their rights to a fair election? So far there was insufficient evidence to overcome a national security argument and see the Gillium store security video.

She spun, her long black robe swishing at her ankles. "Ameri." Her telephone call found him in his office. "I've had a chance to look into the matter you referred to me." Her tone was all business. "I think you're right.

But I am not confident of success. I'll do what I can to raise the issue, but I strongly recommend that you communicate to Allan Hansen that he use the power of the legislative branch to demand answers. Perhaps you can offer to provide him with legal counsel to pursue this matter. It's not like you've never worked in Washington before. Together, we might be able to shine some light on this."

# NINE

## NATIONAL INTELLIGENCE

Blum played the recordings from the cameras the DSA operatives had left in Lauren Bastini's cabin. The video and audio were noise and motion activated. A date/time reading superimposed over the top showed four hours had elapsed between Bastini's departure and the arrival of a car. The cameras and microphones caught the images and sounds of a man and woman dressed in shalwars. The woman wore a traditional Pakistani dupatta over her head and shoulders. They loaded bags and their small children into a car and drove away.

He returned to the hazy images of Bastini. He zoomed as best he could and blew up stills but couldn't tell what Bastini was loading into her car.

A profound sense of remorse mixed with anger and frustration. He was supposed to be a pro at the end of a distinguished career. He'd made mistakes, but none that had put him in shit this deep. Did he still have time to fix his mistakes? If he didn't, his FBI career would be over.

On his direction, the team from the Domestic Security Association had attached a cellular and GPS-based transponder to Bastini's car. They had tracked the Jeep to the Washington Beltway, then lost contact.

Tracking devices were easy to defeat if you knew they were there. He should never have contracted with amateurs.

What a bad operation this had been—bad idea, bad execution. Saying he'd only been obeying orders would make him look weak, like a regretful Nazi after the war. Hansen had shown no signs yet of dropping out of the race. There had been very little mainstream press referencing Hansen's association with the Oakland Four. The story was dropping fast in the right-wing media. The Senate election was too far away to keep the story alive for much longer unless they came up with something new.

If Dalleck wanted to do more to interfere with a federal election campaign, he and the White House could do it themselves or find another stooge.

Bastini was now an active terrorist threat on the loose—the bureau's problem, his problem.

---

In a room furnished with comfortable chairs, and soft lighting, Paul Barstow spoke to his therapist about his affair with Deirdre Owens. He didn't go as far as to say that he'd secretly recorded the encounter on his webcam.

"I let her tie me up, and I . . . well, it turns me on."

"Are you in love with her?"

"No, no. She's older and not my type at all. She works in the other party. We shouldn't be together."

"How did you find each other?"

"At a kick boxing class. It was like she knew. Like I was emitting some kind of pheromone. It's not the image I want to project."

"You find it shameful."

"Yes. Weak. I intend to break it off with her. But when she comes to Washington, we end up in my bedroom with me tied up."

"And you feel helpless?"

"Yes." He lowered his head, averting the man's steady observation of him confessing his impotence with his body language.

"When you surrender control, you are no longer responsible for your actions. You can't get ahead. You can't achieve because you're not in charge."

Barstow nodded. He saw the connection between his feelings of under-achievement. When Deirdre had him tied up, he was not to blame for not getting ahead in Washington, for his feelings of failure.

———◆———

Maybe the therapy had cleared his head. He was getting ahead, or at least trying to get ahead.

He entered the New York Avenue office building for an interview for a job in the Office of the General Counsel of the ODNI.

He kept his head erect. Strong shoulders spread from his neck. *Project confidence. You belong here.*

He'd played lacrosse at St. Paul's Prep and at Williams College. What he lacked in athletic ability, he'd made up for with perseverance. He excelled in teamwork and was ready to give his all to the Office of the Director of National Intelligence.

He cleared security in the lobby and stepped off the elevator into a glass-walled reception area. A young female escort nodded as if in a secret sign to two burly guards and opened a door with a key card. She led him down a hallway whose low ceilings and narrowed walls maximized office space.

A man with an intense focus hurried past, clutching a manila file folder.

Barstow's heart beat faster at the prospect of joining this team. He calmed himself to better concentrate and mentally rehearse his background and why he wanted the excitement and front line action of protecting the nation. If he could work here, his life would be important and meaningful.

The woman left him at the office of the assistant to the deputy counsel.

Greg Thompson, the man who was to decide if Barstow was worthy of a slot in ODNI, had a manner of emphasizing his words with a large head on a thin neck that reminded Barstow of a bobblehead doll. He had the positive manner of someone who knew his importance.

*A good sign*, Barstow thought. He'd done his research and knew that Thompson was nine years older than him and had worked on a Kentucky

Senate race and then the campaign of the president. He was a Schedule C, with no civil service protection but the power of the White House behind him. In another time, Barstow might have worked the *old school* line, but these days that kind of overt elitism was considered bad form. If they worked together, their mutual pasts and intertwined circle of family and friends would come out. Meanwhile, Barstow already felt a level of comfort with him and hoped it was reciprocated.

A lone file rested on a cleared desktop. A silenced screen on a wall was tuned to Fox News. A framed photograph of Thompson in a crowd around the president rested on a bookshelf facing his desk as if always to be in sight when he was working.

Outside, a sharp crack of thunder warned of a nearby lightning strike. Through the tinted windows, the street was so dark it looked like night was falling.

The interview started well, as if Thompson was pitching *him* on why he should work here.

"I think we're just about the luckiest staffers in town," Thompson said with a nasal Southern accent identifiable in the long vowels and soft consonants, grinning mischievously as if getting away with something. "We have pretty much a free hand here, unbound by precedent or law. The legislation creating the ODNI was so vague that we've been forced to feel our way through the regulation-making process." He nodded either at the picture of him with the president or at volumes of the Code of Federal Regulations resting on the bookshelf.

"But then again, we have to explain ourselves to lots of constituents. It's interesting. I promise you that."

Barstow smiled back, eager to work in a place with the freedom to move and improvise.

Thompson tapped his fingers on the file on the desk. "I see you've had some time at Justice. That could be useful. We need to know how they think and how they operate. The press has made a big deal out of the Pentagon and CIA resistance, but it's the FBI who's the big bully on the block. They have lines into every federal, state, and local agency. You think we can get them to see the bigger picture?"

Barstow tried not to appear startled by the sudden referral to his supposed expertise. His job was in the Office of Dispute Resolution. The only contact he'd had with the FBI was a case involving the sexual harassment of a field agent. He nodded as if to confirm his experience. "The bureau is tough, no doubt about it."

"Good, very good. Well, you ready to get to work?"

"Absolutely."

At that moment, an insistent beeping rose. The man's expression changed as he read an alert that scrolled across the screen of a Samsung Galaxy. Fear and apprehension seemed to fill the room. From the hall came the ominous sound of running feet.

Thompson grabbed a multiband radio from the charger on the bookcase. "We have a situation," he said. "Gas." He hurried into the hall.

His body high on adrenaline, eyes scanning, ears searching, ready to fight or flee, Barstow followed Thompson into the hallway.

Three men in gas masks burst out of an office at the end of the passage. They carried a figure in an orange biohazard suit. One man was trying to seal the suit as two lifted and dragged the occupant past Barstow to the elevators. He was a big heavyset man, so the operation was clumsy and comical if not for the dire circumstances.

Beneath the clear mask, Barstow recognized the frightened face of the director of national intelligence, Alex Uberhoff.

Barstow strained to overhear some of the excited short conversations of the staff trailing the director's rush to the elevators.

He heard, "Evacuate–level 5."

An immediate pecking order was discernible among those who wore gas masks and carried thick dark briefcases. They were given immediate access to the bank of four elevators. Men with earpieces armed with MP5 submachine guns followed Uberhoff into the elevator.

Thompson stood with the rest of the expendable staff as the elevator door closed. They might be the luckiest staffers in town, but apparently not considered a critical asset in a gas attack.

Outside, thumping helicopter blades competed with the bleating of police sirens.

Barstow was suddenly conscious of his breathing, measuring, trying to limit his breaths. What was in the air? What unseen agent was about to take all their lives? He'd read of a study that had forecast up to three million people could die if a crop-dusting plane flew across Washington dispersing anthrax.

He followed the man to a stairwell. A woman, mouth and nose covered with a wet rag, shoved past Barstow.

He could feel the panic building on itself, the will to survive imprinted on people's grim expressions. Barstow moved with the panicked herd down ten switchback flights of stairs and through the door marked *Lobby*. Some were sheltering in place, but wouldn't the gas collect inside? *Better to be in the open air*, Barstow thought.

On New York Avenue, people were scrambling out of buildings, some holding umbrellas against the slanting hard summer rain. An accident was blocking part of the intersection with I Street. Drivers were leaning on their horns, driving over a cement divider planted with long fountain grass and stunted azaleas. A helicopter chattered overhead.

He should have known it was only a matter of time before it happened here.

The sounds of jets overhead mixed with a peal of thunder.

An acidic bile rose in Barstow's throat. Was it his fear? Or was it the first signs of chemical poisoning? His clothes were soaked. Was it raining? Or chemical contaminants falling from the sky, dripping into his eyes?

He began to run with the crowd, leaving behind the slow, old, or fat, heading north up 12th Street away from the White House. Flight was futile. He was in the heart of DC. Why had he ever come?

<hr />

"I need information," Director of National Intelligence Alex Uberhoff shouted through the plexiglass covering his face. But no one could hear him. His demand was stifled by the airtight barrier surrounding him and the racket of the helicopter lifting off the roof of the DC office building. All he heard was the Aqua-Lung sound of the filtered air from the hose beneath his chin.

His military aide, Major Pedro Miscalente, his face covered with a gas mask, leaned forward in a jump seat facing Uberhoff, trying to establish a wireless link with his laptop. Two men in gas masks on either side of Uberhoff on the platform seat of the helicopter were part of his security detail that had hustled him out of his office. Maybe they were getting information from the wires in their ears, but Uberhoff doubted it.

As the helicopter banked and lifted off the roof, the director could see members of his staff standing forlornly in the rain. His escape had been well practiced–with a stand-in for him during the drills. He thought this had better not be a drill, then felt ashamed for wishing it was the real thing.

This was it, his first real test. He was the one who was supposed to be getting the information, but he was deaf, dumb, and blind in a helicopter barely large enough to hold five men. How was he supposed to be the central repository of intelligence-gathering operations if he couldn't communicate with anyone?

As they swept over the green banks of the Potomac, he wondered when and how he would learn what had happened. He sat back in the seat as far as the bulky suit would permit. Every minute since the president had offered him this damn through-the-looking-glass job where nothing was as it seemed and everything was topsy-turvy, he thought of something new that had to be changed or modified about his position. Add to the long list a biohazard suit with internal communications capabilities.

He came from a military family who fought in wars in Germany and the United States. He'd been selected for appointment at West Point but had gone to the University of Virginia instead. ROTC at UVA had prepared him for war, but when he'd graduated as a major with the war raging in Vietnam, the Pentagon had decided they had too many majors. He was in business school by then and never got to go to war.

He didn't have a background in security. He'd been brought on because he'd raided and, at least according to his investors, successfully restructured several large corporations. It was hoped he could bring the same efficiency to the intelligence community. Uberhoff found his job to coordinate the eighteen agencies and organizations that gathered intelligence more difficult than any corporation he'd ever reorganized. The agencies hoarded information and competed against each other as if they were on different teams. And when something did go terribly wrong, like 9/11, the response was, *We tried to tell you,* not admitting what they'd done wrong.

The president didn't trust them for good reason. You couldn't fire anyone, and no one ever suffered consequences for wild theories and misguided operations.

No doubt, national security was tougher than commerce. If you suffered a loss in business, you went home and started another business. Here, if you were wrong once, you lost serious real estate and thousands of lives. The pressure to be perfect was constant.

The helicopter flew over his Hunt Country estate where his wife and a maid were alone amid forty acres with a ten-horse herd no one ever rode. He kept an apartment at the Watergate in Washington, so he could be closer to work and not have to deal with her or their children, whose political views were so liberal he could hardly speak to them.

Would they be safe? Would anyone? Fine to save the heads of government, but what about their families?

---

The president had been setting up a golf round with one of his sycophants in the Senate when Secret Service agents rushed into the Oval Office to evacuate him from Washington.

As the presidential helicoptercade flew over the Potomac, west toward the Blue Ridge Mountains, an aide informed him that his wife and son were secure.

The president nodded and stared at his folded hands. What mattered most was that he project strength. Let them think he was praying, not pondering the best way to turn this gas attack into a profitable fundraising appeal.

Twenty minutes after lifting off from the White House lawn, while the decoys carrying the White House staff landed atop the mountain, the president's copter flew into the hanger carved into the granite wall of Mount Weather Emergency Operations Center, the continuity-of-government complex buried in a mountain sixty miles west of Washington. Blast doors closed behind him, and he was safe inside a facility designed to withstand a direct nuclear attack.

Mount Weather was operated by the Department of Homeland Security. Rather than a military base commander and honor guard, the president was greeted by a director of the Federal Emergency Management Agency.

By habit, the president saluted the confused civil servant, who clumsily lifted his open hand to the side of his forehead to return the greeting.

The president's national security advisor, Milo Tooley stepped to his side as they were led to the command center from which the government of the United States could continue to operate for years, if need be.

Tooley spoke calmly, "It looks like a lone strike. Nothing's changed—no reported casualties. There's quite a bit of panic in the city. The Congress and Supreme Court have evacuated to the visitors center."

"What happened?" the president asked.

"Somebody attacked Blue Plains."

"The sewage treatment plant?"

"There was a release of chlorine gas."

With a twinkle in his narrow eyes, the president said, "You're shitting me."

⸻◉⸻

When the threat level went to severe, Blum was one of the first to arrive in the Los Angeles FBI situation room and log in to the National Incident Management System.

*Single MANPAD launch, Blue Plains Sewage Treatment Facility, Washington, DC. Gas: possible Cl. Widespread toxic exposure. Urge citizens to stay inside. Biohazard units respond. Affected areas: Washington, DC, Montgomery and Prince George's County, Maryland; Fairfax and Arlington Counties, Virginia. Confirmed casualties: 0, Projected casualties 21,000.*

The threat level in DC was "Critical." Government officials were being evacuated with the president to MWEOC. All commercial aircraft in the vicinity were grounded or landing at the nearest field. Military aircraft were firing flares and activating antimissile systems.

This could be an isolated incident or part of a synchronized attack. He looked up at a large screen in front of the room and saw no activity in Southern California.

Blum switched to the National Reconnaissance Office's real-time information system, where surveillance from satellites, drones, and blimps was available to commanders for an overview of battles. Washington, DC, was at the top of the list of active combat theaters.

He watched the attack from the perspective of a drone circling over Joint Base Anacostia-Bolling. The cloud cover and rain had no effect on the low-flying UAV. All-weather capabilities showed a flash identified by a computer-imposed map as a point above Interstate 295. A secondary ignition was visible in one-quarter time as the missile flew across the freeway, traveling approximately a quarter of a mile before impacting a target at the sewage treatment facility, causing an explosion.

Blum clicked on the National Security Agency weaponry analysis. NSA identified the missile as an RPG-7VR.

The RPG-7, a single-shot armor-piercing grenade launcher, was a favorite tool of jihadists and terrorists worldwide. There were a hundred suspects who could have attacked Washington with an RPG. Why Blue Plains? Was it a feint intended to draw their attention from another, more deadly attack? Maybe it was just a disgruntled sewage treatment employee.

He viewed the fifteen-minute log of activity after the explosion at high speed. Visible evidence of a person moving away from the launch point was displayed as a distortion framed by a superimposed box. The cameras on the drone recorded what looked like a bag lady getting on a bus.

Whoever had launched the RPG had caught a city bus in the neighborhood above Blue Plains. It would be a poor neighborhood that close to the inevitable stench of a sewer treatment facility. This was from where most of the projected twenty-one thousand casualties would come.

He reached the end of the recorded segment and was in real time. The fact that people were still moving around fifteen minutes after the gas was emitted indicated that it was not deadly or that the wind was blowing in another direction.

The computer framed and tracked seven figures that had gotten off the bus at two stops. Moving $X$'s marked law enforcement units converging on the scene.

Blum watched the bus move along its suburban route. "Stop it," he whispered.

An alert flashed across the main screen and on the individual monitors at the workstations. *Blue Plains: negative chlorine gas. Active agent: sodium hypochlorite bleach.*

The good news was that a toxic gas cloud was not drifting over Washington. The bad news was that whoever had just tried to kill or injure a large portion of the population of Washington was escaping on a city bus.

Blum switched to the Secret Internet Protocol Router Network used to facilitate real-time collaboration and information sharing. He scanned the High-Interest Suspects list for the Blue Plains attack. A Turk who had slipped off a break-bulk ship in Houston was at the top of the list. Blum scrolled down through names with Middle Eastern, Indonesian, and Chinese ethnicities. Lauren Bastini was not on the list.

He didn't want to be right but had a bad feeling that Bastini had gone hot. What the hell had happened to him? He used to stay on top of an operation.

He typed in her name and entered: *Reported contact with Kahlid Shaifqueur, Pakistani arms merchant suspected of smuggling weapons through routes on the Arizona-Mexican border. Possible weapons trafficking: rocket-propelled missiles, machine guns, grenade launchers, and other stolen or surplus US military equipment.*

He attached a picture of Bastini, burn scars snaking around her face like a rock held by purple tree roots, and the DSA video of her loading heavy bags large enough to hold a grenade launcher into a car and the Pakistanis leaving her property.

Law enforcement in DC was seeing what he was. If it was Bastini, there was no way she could escape.

——— ◦ ———

Director Uberhoff's one-piece biohazard suit was highly uncomfortable in the confined cabin of the helicopter. Made of rubberized fabric, his wrists, ankles, and hood were sealed with tight elastic bands, and he breathed through a self-contained breathing apparatus.

The pilots and security detail wore only gas masks, and it occurred to Uberhoff that if he was protected and they weren't to the same extent, what would happen if the pilots were overcome? What good would his biohazard suit do him then?

By the time they landed at Mount Weather, Uberhoff was so uncomfortable and exasperated that he fell out of the helicopter and kicked his legs free like a child trying to get out of a snowsuit.

Major Miscalente and the security detail helped him remove the bio-hazard suit and stand.

The director of national intelligence patted his silver blow-dried hair into place and stared at the FEMA official who'd come to greet him.

"Welcome to Mount Weather," the director greeted him. "The president asks that you join him immediately."

Uberhoff grimly nodded.

The staffer extended his hand across a landing zone crowded with helicopters that had brought other high government officials.

How long had the president been waiting? What the hell could he tell him that he didn't already know? Miscalente had just managed to access the Secret Internet Protocol Router Network through a cellphone hooked to his laptop before they landed.

As he strode across the hanger, Uberhoff demanded out of the corner of his mouth, "What do we have?"

The burly Latino leaned closer and whispered, "It seems to be an isolated incident. They've rescinded the gas alert. Casualties are limited to the facility. FBI has identified a list of seven potential suspects. They think now it was a lone operative. A manhunt is being mounted in the neighborhood where the missile was launched."

"Ahem." Uberhoff cleared his throat, an affectation he'd picked up when he'd been the punter on the University of Virginia football team, as if calling for the ball to be hiked. "I want that list of suspects."

They entered the elevator and dropped into the core of the mountain. Miscalente checked his notebook held before him like a serving tray. "I don't have access to their Wi-Fi."

Did they have their own spot? Shit, he was damned sure that the other agencies were up and running. Did the law prohibiting the Office of the Director of National Intelligence from sharing offices with other security agencies extend to Mount Weather?

The elevator opened, and Uberhoff saw deputy directors of Homeland Security, FBI, and CIA conferring at a workstation in the amphitheater. Uniformed military officers were there. He didn't see any of the cabinet.

A military aide knocked on a door and announced Uberhoff.

"Send him right in."

Uberhoff was escorted into the command center.

Because he gave the president's daily security briefing Uberhoff had grown used to the president's overuse of makeup, his foundation unmatched between his face and neck, unnaturally dark eyebrows drawn on with a harsh outline over panda eyes.

"What's the situation, Alex?" The president held his hands together in front of him on a clean desk.

The vice president and chief of staff sat on either side of the president in seats facing Uberhoff, who remained standing on the hot spot.

He couldn't say he didn't know. He needed time to debrief the other agencies to see what they had. He quickly reported what Miscalente had told him.

"We know all that," the vice president snapped.

"What's the public reaction?" the president asked in a kinder tone as if giving Uberhoff another chance.

Uberhoff thought of his own staff standing forlornly in the rain. "Ahem. There was a level 1 evacuation of key personnel. A public warning was issued in Washington."

The vice president scowled.

The president spoke as if he'd just made up his mind. "Well, if it's a false alarm, we'd better let them know. Sounds like the sewage treatment plant is knocked up pretty good. I want a damage assessment and that facility up and running lickety-split."

Uberhoff didn't say he had no authority or power to repair a municipal facility. That would be FEMA, but they weren't in the room.

"Any idea who did this?"

Uberhoff darted an apprehensive glance at the vice president. "Ahem. There's a short list of suspects. Mr. President. I need to meet with the other agencies and get on top of this."

The president nodded. "We've got a lot of panic on the street out there. I got to get back and try and calm things down. We all might have overreacted."

The president looked away from Uberhoff with a momentary expression of doubt. If they lost the American people's trust, it would be like hurricane warnings–ignored by many in his base who would suffer if they didn't heed the warning of a genuine attack. The tools they needed to stop terrorism would be compromised.

"Find out who did this, Alex. Make it credible. The people need to know who's attacking us." The president stood, and the vice president and chief of staff rose with him.

"Milo. Honcho that meeting."

"Yes, sir," the chief of staff said.

Uberhoff felt relieved. Milo Tooley was his patron. They'd come from the same New York business community.

The vice president stayed with the president while chief of staff Tooley escorted Uberhoff to the outer office. "Please have the directors of DHS, FBI, CIA, DIA, and NSA stand by for a video conference," Tooley ordered the military aide.

Uberhoff nodded at Miscalente, who fell in beside him as Tooley took them into an adjoining conference room. An oval table as large as the one in the White House Cabinet Room had a similar arrangement of chairs along the wall for staff. Screens on the walls projected the same data as the White House Situation Room.

The other directors were in their own secure locations. He wondered what would happen if an electromagnetic pulse knocked out the communication systems. This was why they were all supposed to evacuate to one location. But even if they were all together, what were they supposed to do without telecommunications or contact with the outside world? He thought of Albert Einstein's comment, "I do not know with what weapons World War III will be fought, but World War IV will be fought with sticks and stones."

"I need a password." Miscalente held up his computer to a uniformed officer manning the conference room.

"USA1-$. Wire code along the walls and fully operational workstations at the table." The colonel pressed a button at the side of the table, and a computer screen and keyboard slid up and out in front of the seat.

What kind of password was that? A credit card hacker could figure that one out, much less the North Koreans or Chinese.

"Why don't you sit up there, Mr. Director." Tooley escorted Uberhoff to the far end of the table. "Sorry about the veep," he said softly. "You know he was never supportive of the office."

Uberhoff grimly nodded. This was a test, an important meeting. He was glad Tooley was here to back him up.

"Get me that suspect list," Uberhoff instructed Miscalente.

His aide plugged his laptop into a connection along the wall behind Uberhoff. By the time present staff was seated and the absent directors were on the Zoom for Government array, Miscalente had accessed the Secret Internet Protocol Router Network and was projecting it on the share screen to be viewed by all sixteen participants.

Uberhoff was uncomfortable with his ability to conduct a conference from a grid array and live participants.

"What's the situation?" Uberhoff demanded without identifying who he wanted to speak.

The director of the FBI spoke over the secretary of homeland security.

Technically, the director of the FBI now worked under the secretary of homeland security.

"You go first, Carl," Uberhoff said.

The secretary of homeland security said, "HSAS is level red nationwide. We're going to bring it down to orange nationwide and keep it red in DC. Since the attack was carried out with a MANPAD, we're going to bring air traffic back up more slowly. Initial reports of significant chlorine gas release prompted evacuation alerts. The Cl release has proven false, and I have authorized an all-clear notification. This will assist our manhunt since local law enforcement units will be freed from evacuation and safety duties. We have FBI on the scene, and they are tracking what we believe to be a lone perpetrator."

"Who are you looking for?" Uberhoff pressed.

"Go ahead, Jim," the secretary of homeland security said to the FBI director, James Heikes, a lean former attorney general from New York.

As he spoke, Heikes' aide manipulated the data on the screens. "We are now at thirty-five minutes after the launch," Heikes said.

The main screen projected the infrared feed from the satellite. A clock in the corner spun forward as the director pointed out the superimposed box representing the assailant. "We tagged a lone suspect. Satellite imagery picked up no one else near the launch. We believe the perpetrator boarded a city bus. We have seventeen agents on the scene and detailing all available personnel to the search. We should have several hundred agents on the ground within an hour. It shouldn't be long."

"Who's your top suspect?" Uberhoff demanded.

All eyes went to the HIS list projected on the screen. Each name was color coded from black to red. Lauren Bastini had moved up to number ten, and her name was the reddest.

Heikes said, "One of our agents has given her a strong probability hit. Other suspects haven't received consideration yet. There hasn't been enough time."

"Ahem. Tell us about Lauren Bastini."

Heikes clicked on her name.

Uberhoff's mouth dropped, and he rapidly blinked at the picture of a white, fire-scarred woman in her seventies. She looked like someone you'd want to assist, not a terrorist. What was this all about? What were they dealing with?

As Heikes described Bastini's background, Uberhoff's worry increased. The president was right. They had overreacted. Lauren Bastini was not the type of terrorism the nation had spent billions of dollars and reorganized the government to prevent. This was something new.

Beneath her were grainy images of Shaquat Hailakandi and his family carrying their belongings out of Bastini's honey farm.

"What about the Arab?" Uberhoff asked.

"He's Pakistani," Heikes corrected. "We've identified him as Shaquat Hailakandi, a cousin of Ali Shaifqueur, an arms smuggler with known Lashkar-e-Taiba connections. State Department has tagged Shaifqueur as a Specially Designated Global Terrorist. We have nothing on Hailakandi."

"Ahem. He looks more like what we're looking for," Uberhoff said.

There was some brief hesitation and shared expressions of consternation, but nobody objected to the outright racism of the comment.

"We'll issue a security alert–High-Risk Individual–on Shaquat Hailakandi," the director of the FBI said.

# TEN

## ANARCHY

The attack on Blue Plains had gone better than Bastini had planned until the escape. Pushing a shopping cart, she'd transported the grenade launcher among blankets and stuffed plastic bags along Martin Luther King Jr. Avenue. There had been a time when Congress Heights had been home to working-class people with views of the Capitol and the confluence of the Potomac and Anacostia Rivers. When the main sewage treatment facility for the city had been built, it decimated property values, leaving the foul-smelling neighborhood to the poor and desperate.

She bent over the cart. An olive rain poncho that folds up enough to fit in your pocket covered an Uzi machine gun slung over her shoulder. Workman's gloves covered her scarred hands. A large hat with a droopy brim hung over her eyes. Homelessness and mental illness were not unknown in this neighborhood. She looked like just another unfortunate with her life in a shopping cart. Nobody appeared to be paying attention to her. She'd turned into the yard of an abandoned brick house, roofless, walls charred by a fire that had destroyed what little remained of the structure.

Across the street from the house, a neighborhood group huddled beneath the plastic awning of a bus stop. They didn't act like they had seen the launch blast or explosion or were concerned about the rising smoke behind the hillside. They seemed more interested in trying to stay out of the driving rain.

A red, white, and blue MTD bus was half a block away. Bastini jay-walked across the traffic and was at the end of the line behind a woman who expanded with fat and muscle, holding on to children with both hands, when the first sirens could be heard coming down MLK.

Bastini abandoned the shopping cart, leaving behind the evidence of the attack, and kept her head down when she put her money into the ticket machine. She moved to the rear door and took an empty seat, the only white person on board.

As the bus pulled away, two police cars skidded to a halt in front of the house.

Somebody must have seen the flames from the back of the rocket launcher to trace the source of the shot so quickly. Maybe she'd set the house on fire. If the bus were stopped, she'd stick out like a wild turkey. With her appearance and record, she'd never get out of jail. She'd be noticed if she tried to get off the bus by herself. Maybe blending into the masses had not been the wisest avenue of escape. She should have just popped out of her car, fired a shot, and booked on down the road.

No, there would have been witnesses, traffic jams, and roadblocks. Besides, she wanted the first strike of the new American revolution to arise from the slums.

"Something going on," a teenager said to her friend and looked back toward the police cars. Through the rain-streaked window, smoke was visible, rising over the roof lines.

"What is it?"

"I don't know, drug bust or something."

"Smells worse than ever, don't it?"

"Yeah, I never smelled it so bad."

Nobody seemed to be paying attention to her.

Ahead, the road was blocked by police cars with flashing lights. The sound of sirens came from both directions.

*Don't panic*, she told herself. She'd planned this part poorly.

The two teenagers moved to the rear door.

Was two enough cover? She pushed past the girls and stepped out of the bus as soon as the green light went on.

"White bitch."

"Mothafucka," the girls complained behind her.

Bastini moved down the street, her gaze lowered, and crossed a parking lot to a string of run-down stores into a liquor store.

An Asian clerk sitting behind a wall of plexiglass looked out at her. Nobody else was in the store. Through the beer advertisements on the window, she saw police cars had stopped the bus. Two cops stood beside the rear door with their hands over their guns at their hips.

"You want something?" the man, maybe Korean, asked.

"Give me a lotto ticket," she said, moving to the circular window to push in her dollar bill. "Quick Pick," she said.

He punched the numbers into a green machine. Her eyes darted about. She couldn't wait here. Outside, two men jumped from an unmarked car with communicators in their hands. They were coming straight for the liquor store. *Don't panic.* There wouldn't be a way out the rear.

She shivered, and her hand trembled beneath her raincoat against the cold metal of the Uzi.

The Korean pushed the revolving door between her and him and delivered the ticket.

"Anything more?" he asked.

"No." She grabbed the ticket.

"Good luck," he said.

She turned to face the door. Two plainclothes walked in. Their eyes fixed on her for an instant then searched the store.

"Anybody in here besides you?" one of the cops demanded. The store owner stepped back from the cash register. "My wife upstairs with children." His accent became thicker.

"What's going on?" Bastini leaned against the counter.

The cops studied her. "What are you doing in here?" one asked.

"Buying a lotto ticket." She held up the piece of paper. "Gonna get rich. Get off the street."

"What happened to your face?"

She shrugged. "The street. Rough out there."

"Why you wearing gloves?"

"Hide the scars. Some bastard set me on fire."

The cop frowned and turned back to the store owner. "Mind if we look upstairs?"

"What happen? What matter? You show me police identification," the shop owner demanded.

The plainclothes cop scowled and reached in his pocket for a badge identifying him as DC Police.

The Korean glanced at it through the plexiglass. "What you look for?"

"Mind if we look upstairs?"

"Only wife, baby, and young boy. What you want?"

"Please step out from behind the counter, sir, where we can see you."

The store owner opened the door with a buzzing sound, unsealing him in the bulletproof cage.

"You see anything?" one of the cops asked Bastini.

"Like what?"

"Anybody in a black beard, anyone running?"

"No. I just came out of the rain, bought my ticket to paradise."

"You see anything on the street? See anybody with a rocket?"

Her laugh was an insane trill. "Rocket? Rocket man. I didn't see no rocket man."

The store owner called up to his wife, who came down the stairs holding a baby and leading a young boy by the hand. With lowered eyes, she bowed at the cops.

"You see," the owner explained to the cops. "Only wife and babies." He held his hand out to the stairs. "You want. You go, see."

"Anyone else up there?" one of the cops demanded.

"Only wife, babies." The owner stood in front of his family as if to keep the cops away from them.

The cops looked at each other, the owner, and his family, and back at Bastini.

The front door opened, and some of the passengers from the bus were escorted into the store by a uniformed policewoman who announced in a loud voice, "There's been an accident at Blue Plains. Might be some dangerous gas in the air. Stay off the street. If you start feeling sick, contact the local hospital. They'll tell you what to do. We strongly suggest that you remain indoors until we give you the all clear."

Bastini edged to the rear of the store, trying to stay in the shadows.

The owner herded his family with soft commands into the plexiglass enclosure.

One of the plainclothes officers moved back toward Bastini but stopped at two women in white T-shirts and jeans. "Did either of you see any Middle Eastern men get on or off the bus?"

"You mean like Osama-looking guys?" one asked.

"Or clean-shaven. Dark skin?"

The women looked dubiously at each other as if for a clue about how to answer the question. "Everyone got dark skin around here," one answered and shrugged.

The plainclothes officer looked back at Bastini.

"Rocket man." She giggled.

He glared at her and moved to interview other passengers from the bus.

Outside, the streets and sidewalks were empty. Bastini watched the door, huddled in the rear, her hand under the poncho near the machine gun. She couldn't risk going out alone. She had to hope that the cops' sexism and racism would continue to protect her. Nobody had identified her. She still might get out of this.

An older uniformed officer entered the store. "We've been informed that there was no release of toxic gas. But we strongly recommend that you clear the area as quickly as possible."

Bastini shuffled out the door with her head down, past the gaze of the plainclothes. She moved with the other passengers back on the bus. Traffic was moving again, past the roadblocks. People were out on the streets. The rain had stopped, and sunlight could be seen on the horizon over Virginia.

People on the bus were talking excitedly to each other, shaking their heads, looking out at the street, and asking why terrorists would attack Blue Plains. Nothing like fear to create instant community. People who would never have spoken to each other were coping together with their loss of security.

Bastini stared at her gloved hands. Her goal had not been mass casualties. She'd accomplished what she wanted to sow chaos and fear. The government had used terror to create subservience. She would use the government's paranoia to create anarchy. She would show that one person had the power to bring the beast to its knees. This had been a good start. She had the power. And this was just the beginning.

When Blum walked into the US attorney's office, he found Dalleck and his inner circle of clean-cut young men and women focused on the flat screen in his office, watching the news.

"Andrea, do we have any idea yet who did this?" the commentator asked, looking at the camera with ferocity as if when he found out the answer, he would personally go down and take the sons of bitches out himself.

The reporter, a bleached blonde who looked not pretty enough to be an anchor yet not smart enough to be on the legal talk shows, replied in an earnest, I-wouldn't-tell-you-no-lies voice. "Breaking news, Peter, the Office of the Director of National Intelligence has just released these images of a yet unidentified suspect."

Blum recognized the images he'd uploaded.

"It's clear this was a clever attack by terrorists on the soft underbelly, the guts, if you will, of Washington, DC. The sewage plant . . ."

"Jim . . ." Blum tried to interrupt Dalleck's stretched-neck visual lock on the screen.

The reporter looked like she was positioned at Haines Point, on the Potomac near the golf course where Blum had learned to play many years ago.

"Jim," Blum said more urgently. "I need to tell you something."

Dalleck turned his gaze from the screen and focused on Blum. "What you got, George?"

The big man shifted from foot to foot. "It's confidential."

Dalleck tilted his head.

"About the attack. I need to speak to you in private."

Dalleck snapped his fingers. "Out, everyone out."

The staff members hurried from the room, looking at Blum with heightened interest.

"What do you have?" Dalleck leaned across his desk, speaking in a low voice appropriate for top-secret information.

"The suspect for the terrorist attack is directly tied to Lauren Bastini. I've made all my notes about Gillium and Bastini and . . ."

Dalleck raised his eyes as to heaven with a rapturous smile. He jumped up from his desk and shot his arm out. "I knew it. Goddamn it, I knew it!" His eyes were feverish with excitement. "We were on it. We were ahead of the game. We tried to stop her. We tried to tell them."

Blum could not think how to break through Dalleck's delirium with the sobering thought that Blum, under Dalleck's orders, might be blamed for instigating a terrorist attack on Washington, DC.

Dalleck turned his manic focus to the screen. "How come Fox doesn't know? Why haven't they got it yet?"

"Sir . . ." he used the polite term for his superior by reflex. "I intend to report our actions concerning Bastini. I believe them to be relevant to her activation."

Dalleck's eyes were expanded and darting around the room. He screwed his right fist into the receiving palm of his left like a baseball catcher. "Good, good. Thank you. Yes, it's true. I was on this case! I just wish we had stopped her when we had the chance. We know Hansen sent Deirdre Owens to meet with Jake Gillium, Bastini's coconspirator. It all fits." Dalleck slammed his small, balled fist in his open palm. "Like a glove. We need to get this out. I want every press contact we have, the whole system, to know the background on this story." Dalleck shouted for the staff to come back. "Lawrence! Jane! Get in here!"

"No! We're the reason she went hot. I tried …"

"Good work, Blum! Great work! I've got to get right on this. Don't worry. I'll give you credit where it will do you some good."

As Blum left the office, he thought, *I'm in for the murder of Jake Gillium, now this. What have I done?*

❦

Gradisky's television was tuned to Fox.

An anchor spoke in a somber, ominous voice from a New York studio over the image of Shaquat and his family. "Law enforcement across the country and indeed around the world are searching for the prime suspect, Shaquat Hailakandi. Is this the beginning of a major terrorist attack on the United States? Later we'll talk about what your community must do to protect itself against terrorism. We're going to go live now in Washington, DC, where the all clear has been issued. We're getting our first shots of the Anacostia neighborhood where the attack was launched. Jack Mastanza is on the scene. Jack, what can you tell us?"

"Well, Brooke, I can tell you . . ."

Gradisky's phone rang. He saw it was from the Domestic Security Association.

"Gradisky," he answered crisply.

"Willis, Peta Whiltlison."

Gradisky had been in the business long enough to read the tone of a voice. He knew he was going to hear something hot. He spun away from the television toward his desk and began to take notes.

"How sure are you about your source? And it's FBI? Got it! Got it."

He had already awoken his computer from its slumber by the time he hung up and typed. *Sources high inside the FBI are saying they are looking for a former lover of Senator Allan Hansen as being directly tied to the prime suspect in the rocket attack on the Blue Plains sewage treatment center. As Poliscope reported in issue 533, August 5, Allan Hansen's campaign manager Deirdre Owens . . .*

His fingers danced across the keyboard. He wanted to be first. He had to get this out. This was one of those stories that people would talk about for years; a Democratic senator directly linked to a terrorist attack. It was amazing.

———— ◆ ————

At least they were in a decent copter with padded seats and no biohazard suit. Uberhoff sat beside his aide, Major Miscalente, during the short flight back to Washington from Mount Weather.

So far, the evidence on the ground pointed firmly to Bastini. They'd found the rocket launcher in a shopping cart. DC police had reported a homeless woman with burn scars on her face, matching Bastini's description. She'd been questioned and let go by local cops. Apparently, she'd just caught a bus and rode away.

NSA had talked about "chatter" they were picking up from Arab and Iranian sources. The CIA had tried to go with the Turkish commando, but the best lead so far seemed to be Bastini and the Pakistani, Shaquat Hailakandi.

If Lauren Bastini was the culprit, then they faced as much of a public relations challenge as a criminal investigation. How could they explain to the nation that the evacuation and panic had been caused by a homeless woman who had escaped on a city bus?

Miscalente was monitoring the situation from an open laptop. "Fox is reporting that Lauren Bastini is our suspect," he said.

The director of national intelligence shook his head in disbelief. "But how could they know? We barely know."

Miscalente looked at the computer screen and frowned. "They're also reporting Bastini's connection to Allan Hansen."

Uberhoff pursed his lips and said as much to convince himself as anyone else. "Ahem. I don't care how preposterous this gets. We're going to take it seriously. We're going to treat this as a serious terrorist incident. If Lauren Bastini was the one who did this, then we're going to catch her before she can act again and do more damage."

"Yes, sir," Miscalente said.

"Let's bring in that FBI agent from LA who's pushing her. At least he knows her case," Uberhoff said.

"I'll have him here by tomorrow," Miscalente said.

"Staff all assembled?" Uberhoff asked.

"They're waiting for us at the campus."

The Office of the Director of National Intelligence was too big for the limited office space in Washington. They now shared a large plot with the National Counterterrorism Center at the Liberty Crossing Intelligence Campus near Tysons Corner in Northern Virginia.

"All hands on deck," Uberhoff said, leaning back into the seat. He wondered how the FBI would react to his ordering one of their agents to Washington. Congress had amended the law creating the office of ODNI to limit his ability to transfer personnel from the agencies under him. It would probably cause a small turf war. What a crazy, impossible job this was, he thought for the umpteenth time.

———※———

The last time Deidre had come to his apartment, Barstow had secretly filmed them playing their game. He was in a chatroom that shared and traded videos of that sort to hook up. It wasn't like you could easily find partners other ways. Now, all he could do was pray that their relationship was never revealed.

His cell rang in his Audi R8 audio. He glanced down and saw *Office of the Director of National Intelligence* on the screen. He eagerly instructed the system, "Answer call."

Thompson's voice supplanted the Eagles' "Boys of Summer."

"Sorry our interview was interrupted. Damn nuisance."

Barstow thought of saying something humorous or ironic but only replied, "Yes, it was."

"Anyway, as you can see, we have a lot to do. No time for niceties. Your clearance was transferred from Justice. We need to ask you a few more questions and push your clearance to a higher level. When can you return to my office for further screening?"

Barstow glanced over at the usual Friday morning rush hour stop-and-start on Route 50 in Maryland. "An hour."

"Call me when you get here. I'll have you cleared."

Two hours later, Barstow was in a chair hooked up to a lie detector. He was calm as he went through the questioning, showing no signs of stress.

"Tell us a lie," a woman in a business suit said.

Barstow grinned. "I don't want to work for the Office of the Director of National Intelligence."

"What is the name of your favorite football team?"

"Eagles."

"Do you know Deirdre Owens?"

No way the polygraph wasn't registering an increase in his heart rate and blood pressure. You wouldn't need a machine to detect a lie in his expanded eyes and perspiration over his eyebrows.

The bobblehead Thompson watched the procedure, judging him.

"Yes," Barstow said.

"How would you describe your relationship?"

Jesus, the video, of course they had it. They were in the intelligence business.

He hesitated. *Tell the truth*, he told himself. "Sexual," he said as if calling a ball or strike.

"Do you remain in contact with Deirdre Owens?"

"No," he said.

"Did you discuss classified information with Deirdre Owens?"

Barstow tried to sound lighthearted but heard his response as flippant. "When I knew Deirdre Owens, I didn't know any classified information."

Thompson spoke up for the first time. Barstow had wondered why he was there. "Did she speak to you about government interference in the campaign of Senator Allan Hansen?"

They'd only talked about turning each other on and what she'd do to him if he didn't submit to her. "No."

The interview continued with questions that were obviously irrelevant. No matter what they asked, he could not calm himself. "I no longer have nor intend to have a relationship with Deirdre Owens," he said at the end of the interview, though nobody had asked. He choked down an explanation of his sexual proclivities. Maybe they knew and didn't care. "Guess that's that," he said to Thompson as they walked to the elevator.

"Smart to be forthright about Deirdre Owens. I've seen pictures of her. She looks like a fine piece of ass."

How much did they know? "She was OK, not what I'm looking for," he lied.

"A bit hard around the edges," the man said.

"A bit."

"I'll try and push through your clearance."

<hr>

Leaking to the press was forbidden. Special Agents were warned that they would be fired for going public and liable for obstruction of justice charges if their leaks compromised a prosecution. Sure, J. Edgar Hoover was an infamous leaker, and Mark Felt, "Deep Throat"—the informant who had given the *Washington Post* information about the Watergate investigation—had been the director of COINTELPRO, the original FBI domestic spying and disruption operation. But those leaks had come from the highest ranks of the FBI, not from a grunt like Blum. Everybody in the bureau knew the source of the Hansen story. That Jerry Sabah, assistant director of the Counterterrorism Division, his boss's boss, wanted to meet him in his office on a Saturday afternoon was proof that Blum was in major trouble. No matter how distinguished his career had been, no matter how dutifully he'd served, his FBI career had come to an inglorious end. He was good and fucked.

The taxi left him off at 935 Pennsylvania Avenue. He took the elevator to the sixth floor of the J. Edgar Hoover Building.

Sabah sat behind a polished desk, orderly, everything in place, just like his sculpted black hair. The days of never-out-of-a-suit were over. While Blum wore a jacket, Sabah looked ready to tee off.

"You're the one who leaked the Gillium file from the COPCOM system." It wasn't a question.

Blum had seen too many people get tripped up by their own lies during questioning. If you're going to lie, tell a whopper and stick to it. "I believe the source is the Domestic Security Association."

"I've seen the file of you struggling with Jacob Gillium before he was shot by his mother. You placed a top-secret classification on the file. Why?"

Blum grimly nodded, "Because of Gillium's association with Senator Hansen, I was worried about the evidence being used for political purposes."

"Which it was. Why were you speaking to Mr. Gillium when the struggle ensued?"

Even though he'd known this was coming and had rehearsed various presentations, including laying the blame where it should squarely lay at the hand of US Attorney Dalleck, Blum confessed without hesitation, "I was asking about his association with Senator Hansen and the Oakland Four bombing."

"How did the Domestic Security Association become involved?"

"I was worried about the bureau being perceived as trying to gather information to use against Senator Hansen."

"Which you were."

Blum pressed his lips together. "I see how that could be the perception, as I was detailed to act as an investigator for the US attorney's office."

"Dalleck?"

Blum was glad he hadn't tried to hide anything. Counterterrorism deciphered more complicated plots than this before breakfast.

"I suggested that we outsource the pressure on Bastini. That was a bad idea."

"Bad idea from the start."

"I should have known better."

Sabah looked down at his hands. "This was being directed from the White House. The police file was accessed by Morgan Lancaster, Domestic Policy Council." Sabah looked away from Blum for an instant, then sharply back at him. "There could be a legitimate national security angle to this."

Blum forced his tone of voice to remain neutral, giving information, not excuses, no hint of pleading his case. But he felt his face reddening. "I believe Lancaster leaked the police investigation to gain a political advantage, to defeat Senator Hansen."

Sabah's olive complexion darkened, and he pursed his lips before exhaling. "You talking about dirty tricks? We back to Watergate?"

"More like COINTELPRO." Blum's voice was monotone, not overselling, just confirming a fact.

Sabah drummed his fingertips against the desk. "Talk to anyone else about this?"

"Only Dalleck. I was assigned to his office."

"We've arrested Shaquat Hailakandi because of your DSA surveillance film. Initial interrogation has him as an illegal immigrant. We think he came into the country through the Arizona border. Pakistani intelligence connects him with a cousin, Kahlid Shaifqueur. We don't think Hailakandi is an operative. They don't usually travel with their family. This leads us back to Bastini. She's active because of your bumbling. We think she's a lone wolf."

"Yes, sir. I was worried of this outcome."

"You outsourced the election interference."

"I never liked the idea from the start."

"Your name has been released. How did Deirdre Owens know it was you?"

He exhaled through his nose. "I was recognized by Jacob Gillium. That was why he attacked me. I infiltrated his group in 1986. I was younger then. I didn't think he would recognize me."

Sabah furrowed his eyebrows and frowned. "It is highly likely that Lauren Bastini will share Gillium's anger with you. You could very well be her target."

"I could be the bait that attracts her to reveal herself."

"Yes." Sabah nodded.

Blum thought he still might have a future in the FBI.

Sabah studied him with neither surprise nor condemnation, an expression suitable for when a suspect was making a confession. There was the verdict. Guilty. Even if Blum had not directly leaked the file, he'd shown the way to it, putting the FBI in a position that their enemies could misinterpret and use to limit the bureau's power.

Sabah looked down at a closed manila file, then back up at him. "The White House has asked that you be assigned to ODNI. Find Bastini. No need for outsourcing. Represent the bureau well over there."

"I'll do my very best." Blum turned and left. He was being given a chance to redeem himself. He only knew the theory of the Office of the Director of National Intelligence. He wasn't aware of what resources they had to mount a manhunt. But he intended to do whatever he needed to capture or eliminate Lauren Bastini.

He'd barely reached the street when he was struck by Sabah's comment that the White House had asked for him. He was still a pawn in their game to discredit the campaign of Allan Hansen.

# ELEVEN

## BIG HEADS

The haunted chirp of a pileated woodpecker echoed through the forest. A helicopter droned from the distant border of civilization. Bastini edged forward in the crevice, trying not to expose herself to thermal detectors that might be hovering above.

The rolling hills, dense forests, and rugged terrain of the West Virginia Appalachia offered many hideouts. Bastini's lair was little more than an expanded crevice in the granite that led to a dynamited space in the rocks, large enough for her to store her weapons and survival gear, one of the hundreds of abandoned mines in the region, a remnant of early days when lone prospectors combed these hills looking for an external vein that would lead to black mountain cores of anthracite.

Like a playwright peeking around the stage curtain on opening night, she wanted to know how her effort had been received. She poked the antenna on her battery-powered shortwave into the open air and tuned past the crackling transmissions bouncing off the ionosphere from around the world until she heard a voice with a British accent saying,

"Authorities in the United States have arrested Shaquat Hailakandi, a Pakistani . . ."

The voice faded. Bastini slowly turned the dial but couldn't find more reports about the attack. Poor Shaquat, he'd taken the rap for her. Maybe it would throw them off her trail.

Bastini poked the antenna higher and pressed her head closer to the speaker to listen to the exchange between one of the legions of right-wing radio pundits and an angry caller. Reports of the arrest of Shaquat didn't fool Bastini. They'd be combing these mountains searching for her.

The radio show went to a commercial. She settled back into her nook and leaned against the rock wall. She'd not made the mistake of underestimating her enemy. For two years, once a month, she'd loaded an all-terrain vehicle, hauled a small open trailer loaded with supplies and boxes of weapons up the steep slope, lurching over rocks across stream beds, knowing this day would come.

Nobody who'd known her or had worked with her would be able to provide any leads. Sally, the girl who ran her store, had been told Bastini had gone to Indiana to visit her mother. Bastini had grown up in Riverside, California, and her mother had been dead fourteen years. They might narrow their search to this mountain, but they would have to get damn lucky, or else she'd have to be careless for them to find her. And if they did, she was ready to take a few of them out with her.

She slid down the rocky slope into the dank cave and crawled onto a bed she'd made on the dirt floor to wait until it was time to launch the next salvo in her war on the pillagers of nature.

———◦———

Uberhoff had instructed that special agent Blum be included in the Zoom for Government meeting. End-to-end encryption and secure user authentication safeguarded the meeting from unauthorized access.

The usual bowlful of threats from around the world was on the agenda of the reps of the multiple intelligence agencies Uberhoff allegedly coordinated. The active domestic terrorist focus remained on the Blue Plains rocket attack. Four days since someone had fired an RPG at the sewage treatment facility, and no evidence had emerged to change the focus of the investigation from Lauren Bastini.

After the 8:00 a.m. Monday meeting, a car was waiting to take Uberhoff to the White House for the president's daily security briefing. He would have to tell the president that the arrest of Shaquat Hailakandi trumpeted on the news was only a palliative. The probable perpetrator, an old American white woman, was still at large and probably planning more acts of terrorism.

Blum was seated at the table with Uberhoff and his top staff. Each participant had their own computer and image displayed on a grid.

Uberhoff looked at the special agent, concentric darkness under his eyes, hair like sand on a beach a wave had passed, and silently prayed the battle-worn veteran had a plan to capture this old hippie.

"Blum, what do we have on Bastini?" Uberhoff directed the focus to him.

Blum lowered his head as if to see more clearly. "I believe that Bastini is hiding in the mountains near her home in West Virginia. I think we should search there."

The FBI liaison at ODNI had a weary seen-it-all voice. "It took us five years to get Eric Rudolph, the Olympic Park Bomber. He survived in a small valley, nearly invisible. A rookie police officer caught him rummaging through a dumpster."

"Ahem. We'll do better," Uberhoff said, without knowing how they would do better. He wasn't going to back down now. "I want all resources thrown into this hunt, manned and unmanned surveillance aircraft, satellite, military, civilian, the works."

The CIA liaison, Krisky, a woman Uberhoff ordinarily found intelligent and reasonable, took the last stab at dissuading him. "What makes you think she's still there?"

Uberhoff looked at Blum, who seemed not to want to speak over Krisky.

"If she'd not gone to ground," Blum said, "we would have picked her up by now. She's been planning this for a long time. This is her turf. This is where we'll find her."

Good man. Uberhoff gave him a quick nod, then glowered at the rest. "Let's get to work, people. Let's find Lauren Bastini." He adjourned the meeting and signed off the Zoom. Blum exited the conference room with the rest of the staff.

"Ahem. Greg, stay a minute, will you?" he said to the bobblehead assistant to his deputy counsel.

The lawyer lingered as the others filed out of the room. "I want you to assign that new lawyer we just hired, what's his name?"

"Paul Barstow."

"Pair him up with Blum. These agencies are going to resist giving us anything more than lip service. I want Barstow to throw the law at them. We have the law on our side. Congress gave us this power. We have to use it or lose it."

The aide nodded grimly, started to leave, then turned back. "You should know that Barstow may be compromised."

Uberhoff looked up from the president's briefing file.

The aide leaned forward and said in a gossipy, almost smarmy tone. "We picked up an intercept from him on Deirdre Owens's phone."

"Who is Deirdre Owens?"

"She's Senator Hansen's campaign manager."

"Are we spying on a political campaign? Who ordered the intercept?"

"The White House, Morgan Lancaster, Domestic Policy Council."

"He's one of their politicos, isn't he?"

"Yes, sir, came off the president's campaign staff."

"Ahem. I don't like this. I don't like this at all. The attorney general issued two directives prohibiting the FBI from spying on political campaigns. Did they go to court, get a FISA warrant?"

"I don't know."

"I'll bring it up with the president. Now what's this about the new lawyer? I brought him on to work on this case."

"He's had an intimate, perverted sexual relationship with Deirdre Owens."

"Did she say anything about Bastini?"

"Not to Barstow, but she did speak to others about Bastini and her relationship to Senator Hansen."

"Present relationship?"

"Not that we can tell."

"Why are we intercepting the calls of a campaign manager?"

The aide leaned closer, propping his right arm on the table, and said, "Fox is reporting . . ."

That was all Uberhoff had to hear. He exploded. "Ahem. Then why don't we all just watch television and get out of the intelligence business? I want facts, goddamn it! I don't want rumors, innuendo, or scandal. Facts!" he seethed. "Do I make myself clear? Facts!"

The aide nodded.

"Do we have any evidence that the campaign manager is a security risk?"

"No, it's political. It's the senator they suspect."

"I don't like this, not at all," Uberhoff repeated. "Nobody on our team is to engage in surveillance not directly tied to an identified risk without a lawful warrant. Unless we have a reasonable suspicion that Senator Hansen or anyone associated with him is conspiring with her or in contact with Lauren Bastini, I want hands off. Hands off."

"I'll prepare a directive."

"Keep us out of this. It's nasty business, politics, not national security. I want our hands clean."

———◦———

What set Gradisky apart from the other hacks was his ability to get more. He paused over the story he was typing. The Hansen-Owens-Bastini story had legs, lots of legs. It was a stomping millipede it had so many legs. On Saturday had come the tidbit–from the same source at DSA–that an intercept on Deirdre Owens's phone had been from Paul Barstow, a political appointee in the Justice Department. A bit of digging and he found that Barstow was being considered for a job in the Office of the Director of National Intelligence. He needed something more explosive before he ran with this. Deirdre Owens fascinated him—enough to get on a plane to track her down.

———◦———

Tuesday morning outside the Commonwealth Club, a cool breeze blew from the bay across the Embarcadero in San Francisco. Deirdre stood to the side of Hansen as he spoke to the press about his opposition to the Sentinel Act.

The proposed law would require all Internet and phone services to provide the government with a "golden key" to decrypt communications. The proponents of the law argued that law enforcement and national security analysis needed to be able to intercept and listen to communication to fight terrorism and child abuse. An interesting development was that some of the most conservative senators had joined the opposition because of what they said was political bias in the FBI against the president.

Hansen was opposed because he said there was no way the back door could be limited to *good guys*. He pointed to the loss of a National Security Agency tool to break into computers as proof that no golden key could be protected from use by cybercriminals.

A female reporter who looked like she'd played college sports, strong and ready to kick a ball, turned her cell toward Deirdre. "You're Deirdre Owens, aren't you?"

Hansen stepped back as if to give Deirdre more space or to get out of the shot.

"Yes."

"Were you in direct contact with Lauren Bastini or any of the coconspirators of the Oakland Four?"

This was a bushwhacking. The LAPD transcript had her name. "I visited with a supporter of Senator Hansen, a man Senator Allan Hansen helped send to prison by interrupting their terrorist scheme while in college. Jacob Gillium had come to recognize, as so many others, particularly those that Senator Hansen has the honor of representing in California, that Senator Hansen is a hardworking, clear-thinking servant of the people who is working tirelessly to protect the people of the United States in all regards. The Sentinel Act would allow the government to listen, read, or see ..."

"Deirdre, what is your relationship to Paul Barstow?"

She knew that friendly, almost-familiar voice. It was Gradisky. Deirdre's focus shot to him. He looked like someone she might have gone to college with at Beloit—sure of his intellect, smug, and casual. He held up a cell, recording her reaction. His half smile had the sadistic pleasure of a stalker, an expression that seemed to say, *I'm watching you. I know everything about you.* The feeling of being observed, of a complete lack of privacy, caused her to blush with embarrassment.

Her eyes darted back to the lenses of the cellphones. "Today, nameless bureaucrats and law enforcement officials have the power to see and release confidential information . . ."

Gradisky blew on the embers of the story. "Is that what happened with the LAPD crime report? A mother tragically shoots her own son and says he was struggling with someone sent by Senator Hansen."

Fury rose in her at his smirk, the way he played with the tragedy as a hatchet to attack Hansen. The words rushed from her before she could control herself. "Yes, as a matter of fact, it is. It is my understanding that a grand jury in California is going to be investigating whether the so-called COPCOM system was accessed for illegal purposes in order to release police reports . . ."

She stopped. Her throat tightened. She stared at the lens of the cell. Battlestone had asked her not to talk about a grand jury investigation of the release of the LAPD evidence. She'd requested Hansen not to mention it.

Now that she had made the COPCOM release public, Hansen was off to the races talking about federal government interference with his campaign. He hoped that the grand jury would find enough evidence ... how the Senate should be investigating and subpoenaing . . .

She'd compromised Battlestone and, worse, the secret proceedings of a grand jury. Whoever was putting together the investigation would now be subject to interference by those they were trying to investigate. If the leak of the Gillium transcript had come from the Justice Department, they now had been placed on full alert by her idiotic remark.

Gone in a flash was her self-image as a pro.

The revelation of real news prompted questions from the reporters.

"Where is the grand jury?"

"Is it a federal grand jury?"

"Has anyone been notified that they are under investigation?"

"Have any target letters been sent?"

"Who has been subpoenaed?"

She swallowed hard, stepped back, and summoned the will to counterattack.

Hansen appeared to relish the opportunity to speak openly about the nascent investigation. "My understanding is that the grand jury will be investigating whether the FBI's Counterintelligence Unit has actively interfered with an ongoing political campaign." He recited Battlestone's argument. "Once the executive branch attempts to subvert the election of a member of the legislative, we have cut to the heart of the US Constitution. If we accept this act, even the possibility of this act, then we overextend and risk rupturing the balance of power, which is the soul of the Constitution."

"Deirdre, what has this done to you personally?" Gradisky asked, barely able to keep from breaking a grin. He had stepped close enough to reach for her.

The absurdity of the question in the context of the seriousness of the topic caused her to shoot him a look of contempt and anger, unfortunately also directly into the lens of his cell.

"That's all we have time for today," she said as if she was running the show.

As they entered the building, Hansen was upbeat. "I'm glad you put that out there. Frees me to talk about it."

*My fault. Stupid. My fault.*

"I fell into a trap, lost my mind."

"Since the press is so interested in you, I want you to push forward. Do the rounds. If there's no grand jury investigation, then there should be one."

Great, was she now supposed to be a freak on display? *Miss BDSM is here to discuss ...*

———⊙———

Barstow sat in the passenger seat of the car they'd rented at Dulles Airport using Blum's credit card. The speed of his life was increasing, and the pure excitement of his job after the dreary year in the Department of Justice thrilled him.

Hunched slightly over the wheel, steering with one hand, driving too fast, passing cars on the right, Blum said, "Tell me about Deirdre Owens."

The suddenness of the question surprised Barstow as if a brick had landed on the windshield. How many people in ODNI knew about his predilection for being restrained by a lover? He glanced at the profile of the man's large head. "Deirdre?" He stalled to know the context of the question.

"Senator Hansen's campaign girl."

Deirdre had been asked about him at a news conference that morning in San Francisco. What would he tell his family if the video went public of him being tied to a bed and whipped? He was ruined. He'd done it to himself.

"Yeah. She's a freak, into bondage."

The man's gaze turned to him too long to have his eyes off the road.

Barstow felt like he was being interrogated again. "I was with her a few times. How do you know her?"

"It's my business to know things. She ever talk to you about the bureau?"

"The FBI?"

"Yeah."

Barstow's voice rose with anger and indignation. "Look, what is this all about? I had a thing with an older woman. Is that a crime?"

"I couldn't give a rat's ass about what you do in the sack. She's an enemy of the bureau and has the senator's ear. He's going around saying the bureau is messing with his campaign."

119

"I understand she and the senator have made those claims publicly."

Blum's voice was a growl, heavy with age. "Might have to do something about her, him. That's why I'm on this case. We'll find this bitch up here and roll her up to Hansen."

What did that mean? Deirdre's suspicions about the FBI playing dirty seemed all too real. Was he now supposed to join Blum's crusade to defend the FBI? "What do you expect me to do about it?"

"Why did they send you?" Blum asked with a dollop of scorn in his voice.

"Throw some law at them."

Blum sadly shook his head.

Barstow thought of saying something macho about bringing a knife to a gunfight but held his tongue.

"Think they'll pass the Sentinel Act?" Blum asked.

"I don't know," Barstow said.

"The bureau needs access to electronic communications. Nobody ever outlawed wiretaps. I know you need a warrant," Blum said. "Went to law school myself."

"Oh." Barstow couldn't keep the surprise out of his reaction. He'd figured Blum had come out of the military.

"They can use Section 702, can't they?" Barstow referred to the Foreign Intelligence Surveillance Act.

"Yeah, but now they're likely not to reauthorize it, and if they do it's going to place limits on intercepting the calls of American communications. Don't always have time to go to FISA for a warrant," Blum said.

"Too bad we didn't have Bastini under surveillance."

Blum's angry frown alerted Barstow that he'd touched a nerve.

With a quick cough, Blum confessed. "We did. That's why I'm on the case. Have to find her. My mistake."

Barstow waited for Blum to tell him what he'd done or hadn't done, but the old agent remained lost in his seeming remorse, his lips pressed together in consternation.

Barstow wondered what traumas were driving Blum. Deirdre didn't mean anything to him. He'd set her up if the job required it. Maybe he should volunteer to entrap her. But he thought better of doing anything more to associate himself with her.

———◦◉◦———

Anthony Belligoni was called into Hillary Morgenstern's office the minute he reached work at seven forty-five, Wednesday morning.

Morgenstern was the United States attorney for the Central District of California. She had been appointed by the president last year and had only been confirmed by the Senate six months before.

Technically, Belligoni worked for her, but as one of 260 assistant US attorneys, he rarely had direct contact with her. Most of the business of operating the office was done by assistant US attorneys like him.

Serious beyond her years, as if to compensate for being an attractive young woman, and with a supercilious smile as if to say, *Isn't this something?* She was dressed in a court-appearance-ready matching jacket and skirt. A pearl necklace, as if a nod to her gender, hung from her slender neck. She demonstrated legal prowess while attending a good law school, clerking for a federal judge, and serving as a California state judge. But the reason she oversaw the largest U.S. attorney's office outside of Washington, DC, was because she was a good politician and had chosen the right party. She was the voice of the White House and attorney general. Her large office was somewhat ceremonial, with flags, pictures, sitting areas, and a conference table. She came around the desk smiling like the mayor of a small town, her hand extended. "Tony, it's good to see you again."

They sat at the conference table, Belligoni on one side of her and Dalleck on the other. Dalleck's reputation was pure politics, with little experience prosecuting cases.

"I've admired your work. I'm glad to have this chance to work directly with you," Morganstern said.

"Thanks. Likewise." He tried to act comfortable, placing his hands on the table and leaning back in his seat.

Her manner became more serious as her smile faded. She looked at him while he kept his eyes focused on his hands. "I was reviewing your authorization memo about the COPCOM investigation."

An authorization memo stated the violation, the suspect, and how the grand jury would be used. It was a pro forma first step almost always approved. He should have known.

"Did you release that memo to anyone, Tony?" Her tone was not accusatory, but he instinctively went into an adversarial mode, guessing that someone had leaked the investigation. "No." His jawline hardened, and he returned her stare.

"You know what's the first thing I got when I came into work today? Lots of press inquiries about whether we're investigating Senator Allan Hansen. Are we?"

If she had read the memo, she should know it was only tangentially about Hansen.

"Upon what are you basing the allegation of FBI interference with the senator's reelection campaign?" Morgenstern asked as calmly as if inquiring about a restaurant he'd gone to last night. "Where did this information come from? I don't see anything in the authorization memo about the source of the information." She looked back up at him, her stare hard, unwavering.

Had anyone else asked him, he could have said he needed to protect his sources, but he couldn't dodge this one. "The information was referred to me by Judge Wallace."

"Ah, Judge Wallace." Morgenstern raised the corner of her lip.

He might as well have revealed that the Democratic National Committee had given him the tip. In Morgenstern's political world, Wallace was from the other camp. He had just confirmed her suspicion that this was a political trap set for the administration.

He leaned forward in his chair. "The information about who accessed the COPCOM file has been classified. I sought the authorization memo in order to proceed with a CES referral." In other words, he needed the memo to begin the process of accessing classified information for possible criminal prosecution.

"And you assumed the government would not offer a suitable substitute of the information?"

"I wanted to see. Let them tell us who accessed the file and released the information. It seemed like a flimsy national security screen to me."

"What makes you think so?"

"It just didn't seem to fit the facts. I think somebody is hiding something."

Morgenstern exchanged glances with Dalleck and turned her gaze to him. "I'm going to turn this over to Dennis. He has more experience with national security issues."

Belligoni couldn't stop a disparaging huff from escaping his chest as anger rose in him. It had become a joke the way this administration cloaked embarrassing political problems in national security.

Her eyes hardened and froze on his. "Please turn over the file to Dennis."

"I'll need a complete debrief," Dalleck said.

"It's in the charging memo."

"I saw no mention of the allegation that pressure was being put on the victim by someone sent by Senator Hansen," Dalleck volleyed the shot back from the White House court to switch the focus.

Belligoni looked at the man and thought, *Just how stupid are you?* "I haven't seen the COPCOM file. Have you?"

Dalleck shifted in his seat and replied too quickly. "Just what was in the news."

"That's the point, isn't it? That it was in the news?" Belligoni asked.

"We have to see, have to see," Dalleck repeated. "Have you uncovered any evidence of a third party or federal government interference?"

"Just what I'm hearing now."

"All right, that's enough innuendo," Morgenstern snapped. "May I remind you that you serve at the pleasure of the president?"

Belligoni twisted his lips and nodded.

"And you might want to remind Judge Wallace and anyone else who might have access to this information that grand jury investigations are to be conducted in secret."

His jaw clenched. This was not the time or place to argue. The misuse of the COPCOM system was all political now, beyond the realm of a grand jury investigation. If anyone asked, they would be told there was no grand jury investigation. Anyone wanting an investigation of the COPCOM system would have to go through the attorney general's office.

"Thanks for coming to see me, Tony." She stood.

"Later," he said and left the office. He figured correctly that he would be fired by close of business.

---

Judge Wallace had difficulty keeping her attention on the handwriting expert testifying on a forgery of a contract signature. The public announcement of a grand jury investigation by a sitting US senator, her senator, could only be laid at the feet of Ameri Battlestone.

The line between politics and law was not as neatly drawn as the separation of powers between the legislative and judiciary branches of government. There was nothing new about politicians trying to incite or influence legal action, but she didn't like being used to make a political statement.

As soon as the witness was done, Wallace banged her gavel and announced a half-hour recess. She hurried back to her chambers, fell into her desk chair, and picked up the phone.

She barely paused to greet Battlestone before launching into her complaint. "I won't be pulled into a political whirlpool."

"It was naïve of me." His deep voice was remorseful. "The question is, where do we go from here? I am sure you agree there remains sufficient cause to investigate."

"Well, it won't be through the US attorney's office. I can tell you that. This administration is not eager to investigate itself."

"Then you think the culprit is to be found in the administration?"

She shifted in her seat and leaned toward the window.

"Ameri." She spoke in a kind tone as if trying to explain something to a dutiful student. "What if there is a genuine national security issue? From what I am hearing about the senator's involvement with Jacob Gillium, there is probable cause to launch an investigation."

"You raise another point precisely. How do we know it is Lauren Bastini who attacked Blue Plains? The FBI has managed to directly tie Allan Hansen to a terrorist attack on Washington."

"With the loosest of association," Judge Wallace agreed.

"How is it that the FBI confirms that Jacob Gillium's coconspirator in the Oakland Four is their prime suspect?" Battlestone asked. "Our elected officials cannot be shielded from the genuine investigations of behavior."

Judge Wallace agreed, "The framers knew well the importance of legislators being shielded from the threat of legal persecution."

"In the furtherance of their duties as legislators. I still believe what we have here is an attempt by the FBI to interfere with a domestic election. If anything, I am more convinced of the need to expose this abuse of power and see that it is not allowed to mutate and grow into something worse."

"Oh, there is a cover-up here. If they think that I won't hear evidence of their scheme, they have mistaken me."

"Who will bring the evidence?"

"In their clumsiness, they have also revealed their doings to the federal attorney I asked to look into this. They have fired him, and as of today, he's employed by the Alliance for Justice and preparing a Freedom of Information Act lawsuit."

"The path is never straight but bends to justice."

"Imagine your clients love that poet soul of yours no matter whom you cop from."

"You don't?"

"You know I do."

<hr />

Morgan Lancaster sat behind a mahogany desk positioned near large, arched windows with a view of Lafayette Park.

His concerned pair of mismatched eyes, the right in a squint, scanned the latest Poliscope entry and he rubbed the back of his hand beneath his nose.

*Political consultant Deirdre Owens announced today a grand jury investigation into the leak of an evidence report by the LA Police Department. Her client, Sen. Allan Hansen, was directly associated with the Oakland Four, a radical eco-terrorist group. Repeated inquiries for details to Hansen and judicial sources reveal no grand jury details, leading one to believe that the whole idea was a fabrication by Hansen to deflect attention from the core issue. Was he a Berkeley radical in college, and is his old gang still active–perhaps to blame for the Blue Plains attack last Thursday in Washington, DC? Owens will appear on* The EDGE *tonight, and one assumes she will be asked to provide more info on her charge that the COPCOM system was used illegally to subvert the uphill Hansen reelection effort.*

Lancaster smirked. Large ears hung like wings from a prematurely bald head elongated as if pulled from the womb with some internal resistance.

*Uphill*, indeed; he'd been vindicated. How could he get credit for what he'd done? The story of how he'd single-handedly detected and attempted to counter a terrorist attack on Washington could be his making. He was the one who had been orchestrating the revelation of Allan Hansen's deep involvement in terrorist activities. Willis Gradisky from Poliscope was his puppet dancing on the strings of information he'd been feeding him through the Domestic Security Council. Technically and by law, Lancaster was an employee of the US government. He wasn't supposed to be coordinating political activities with a conservative think tank. But all was fair in love and war and, in his mind, politics.

Still, this talk of a grand jury investigation was worrisome. What was his exposure?

He opened the COPCOM system, and his eyes went to the small print on the opening page, and he quickly rubbed the itch on the tip of his nose.

*Whoever knowingly accesses without authorization or exceeding authorized access, and by means of such conduct obtained information for unauthorized disclosure, is subject to a fine under this title or imprisonment for not more than twenty years . . .*

An acid burn rose in this throat. His eyes watered. Twenty years. He pulled his fingers like a vise down his nose.

He stared at the log-in line where he had typed his password to access the COPCOM system. Panic and remorse swept over him. This could be a massive scandal. The kind that goes on for years. The legal costs could financially ruin him—jail or not.

The system would surely have a traceable audit trail. He'd entered his name and password to look at the file he'd shared with the Domestic Security Council. They were the ones who released the files to the press, not him. The FBI could be coming to arrest him, walking down the hall.

He would deny the allegation. Systems could be hacked into. He might even insinuate that it was a computer hacking job designed to embarrass the administration. He just needed DSA for cover.

"Mr. Branson's office," a perky female voice answered.

"This is Morgan Lancaster at the White House. I need to speak to him immediately."

"I'm sorry, Mr. Lancaster, Mr. Branson is in a meeting . . ."

"This is urgent. I need to speak to him now!"

"Wait a minute, please."

He cupped the phone against his shoulder to rub his nose and drummed his fingers against the desk. He loved having the power to say he was from the White House. What would that do for him in jail? He'd have to hide his background, act tough, and maybe join a prison ministry.

"Morgan?"

"Jim, we've never talked about anything to do with Hansen, did we? I'm hearing some faint rumblings of an investigation, and I think we need to make it clear right from the start that nobody from the White House was involved."

"Morgan, I'm sorry. I don't know what you're talking about." Branson sounded sincerely perplexed.

"Good, me either. Let's keep it that way."

Lancaster's head sunk toward his desktop. The deep state could put a lot of pressure on someone. He doubted Branson was strong or personally committed enough to the cause of defending the White House. He leaned back in his leather-backed chair. DSA was not going to cover for him. All he could hope for was that the trail did not lead to him.

———◦◉◦———

Jerry Sabah, assistant director of the Counterterrorism Division, was working at his computer on an email to the Office of Professional Responsibility.

*Investigate and report immediately to me all access to the COPCOM system re: Jacob Gillium, Los Angeles Police Department transcript, and related files.*

His secretary buzzed him and announced that the attorney general was on the line. Sabah stared at the phone. He rarely got direct calls from Raymond Patterson. There were too many deputies and directors between them.

"Jerry Sabah," he answered in a military reporting-for-duty voice.

"Jerry, how are you?"

"Very well, and how are you, sir?"

"Couldn't be better. Listen, Jerry, this COPCOM thing, the release of the police report about Senator Hansen, has some serious implications."

Sabah pulled in his lower lip. His political superiors came and went with each administration. He stayed. The bureau followed its own conscientious course. Some of the Schedule Cs shared their political strategies with him, and some did not. But he had never had an attorney general call him about a possible crime.

The attorney general made his pitch like the politician he was. "You know, we are in some very serious late-stage negotiations with the Senate on the Sentinel Act. We're starting to hear from some of our friends up there that they are not comfortable with the possibility of domestic counterintelligence activity in our elections. We need the Sentinel Act. We don't need evidence of FBI meddling in a political campaign."

Everybody with Sabah's years of service remembered or had heard the stories of when the Senate had last clamped down on the bureau after the Church hearings. He fully shared the AG's concerns.

"We need to take our time with this," the AG said. "I want a full internal investigation, and if need be, I'll consider appointing a special counsel."

The longest possible route.

"I agree," Sabah said. And he did.

"Send me the file. My office will handle the investigation."

---

Deirdre had fantasies about being a television personality. Plenty of political consultants had appeared on talk shows, and a few had made it to the host level. For all the times she'd been in the studio with a client, she'd never been under the lights. She was the client now. She needed to be prepared to enter the media gladiator pit where retired majors explained battle tactics and proponents of peace were exposed as hapless innocents.

She met Annie Metcalf, a media consultant, in her LA office on Wilshire. They sat in a small glass-enclosed conference room in a minimalist, open-plan office, natural light streaming in from large windows.

Metcalf, a woman with a small turned-up nose, appeared to look at Deirdre in amusement.

"Let's go over your relationship with Paul Barstow," she said.

"Why?"

"It's the human-interest angle. You're going to be asked about it."

"It's casual."

"Can you make it more? You know, Montagues and Capulets, opposites attract."

"I'd rather not."

Metcalf looked down at an open laptop and raised her blue eyes.

"It's on the dark web. He's tied up on a bed. You've got a crop whip."

"Not me."

"The Christian Right wants to save you."

"There is no privacy left, is there?"

"Not in politics."

"Can you tell it's me?"

Metcalf flashed a moment of embarrassment and looked down and then up at Deirdre. "Not clearly. Probably was shot with a webcam. I take it you didn't consent to being filmed. You can either deny or run with it. It'll gain sympathy for our main point that privacy is under attack, tie into the senator's opposition to the Sentinel Act."

That was a stretch. This was about an egotistical pervert who wanted to film himself in action. Deirdre pulled her cheek into a grimace and shook her head. "No, that won't fly. Better to leave it alone."

Metcalf moved on. "Wardrobe and makeup, going to be hot up there. You'll be up against Mary Regina. Bet she'll wear black. Good girl look for you. Work with the chest up, eggshell blue to white, wide-collared, open neck, show a little skin, little plunge, not too much, necklace something thin, dull, nothing flashy."

"Could this be more sexist?"

Metcalf cocked her head. "You could wear a suit."

Deirdre raised her cheeks and eyebrows. "How 'bout a full-leather dominatrix?"

"Rip off your suit to reveal Supermama." Metcalf bent over with laughter.

130

Deirdre had broken through the professional demeanor. She'd scored a sister.

———◦❀◦———

Deirdre and Metcalf were greeted by a production assistant, a young woman who escorted them past the set from which Roger Hartman conducted his interviews and *leveled* with his viewers. The air inside seemed heavily cooled, contrary to what Metcalf had said.

Deirdre was led into a small makeup room where Mavis, a pleasant-looking Black woman, was ready with her tools. Deirdre sat in a padded, adjustable chair. A ring light was shined on her face, and Mavis went to work with her foundations, concealers, primers, blushes, bronzers, highlighters, eyeshadows, eyeliners, mascaras, lipsticks, lip glosses, and hairspray.

"Now, calm down. You're going to do fine," Mavis said and pressed a terry cloth sweat pad against Deirdre's forehead.

"May I have some water?"

Mavis opened a small bottle and handed it to her.

Deirdre took a sip, but her throat immediately dried. Feeling inept and unprepared, how was she going to speak? She trembled in the chair and wanted to stand. This was her fault; she needed to put her life where her mouth had taken her. The White House was orchestrating criminal interference in a domestic political campaign. She had to call out the alarm.

A woman Deirdre had often seen on conservative media swept into the room followed by an anxious aide clutching a file folder.

"Hello, Mary," Mavis greeted her.

Mary Regina, dressed in a sleeveless black leather dress that seemed way too hot for an August day and showed off well-defined biceps, looked like someone who would enjoy holding a whip.

"Hello, Mavis. How much time do we have?" she barked in a familiar authoritarian voice.

"Plenty of time."

"Well, do my hair, straighten it out a bit, will you? God, this humidity. It gets too fluffy. I look like I have a bouffant."

Her hair looked like a blond helmet on a thin stand of neck and shoulders. Hard to imagine it fluffy.

"Ha ha," Regina laughed and looked at Deirdre as if to share a girl joke.

Deirdre did not return her smile. *I'll show you how to wear leather.*

Regina's eyes hardened. "Give me the file," she ordered her assistant.

Deirdre and Mavis exchanged glances.

"You look fine," Mavis said. "Why don't you go into the green room? They have food and drinks there. Relax."

Excess makeup rested heavily on her face. Her hair felt like a cardboard hat.

Metcalf was waiting outside the makeup room. "I just got word the *Times* and *Post* are going to be running articles on this tomorrow. This could be the late-summer scandal. They're hungry as wolves in winter."

"Allegories running wild; no matter the season, I'm the tethered goat," Deirdre said, laughter breaking her tension for a moment.

The production assistant led them to an enclosure at the edge of the stage. Inside was a lounge with a television tuned to the studio feed of an empty desk. A table with a floral display held a plate of sandwiches, fruit, candies, and drinks—what you might find in the back of a hotel meeting room.

Deirdre had barely looked around when Roger Hartman burst in.

"Deirdre Owens," he growled as she faced him as if to defend herself from an attack.

His head looked freakishly big, resting like a lampshade on mismatched shoulders. He pumped her hand and leaned over her. "This is going to be rough, but it's going to be fast, the fastest five minutes of your life. Don't lose your breath. Breathe. Breathe. Breathe." He imitated the function as if she was a mermaid cast on the shores of his strange land.

He was gone as fast as he promised her appearance on his show would be.

An assistant director came in wearing a headset attached to a box on her waist. "Ready?"

Deirdre's legs felt wobbly. She was sweating through her makeup and blouse. The lights over the stage were as hot as a heat lamp and impossibly bright.

Metcalf walked beside her, giving last-minute instructions. "Camera with the red light is live. Eye on the director for cues. Watch out for Regina. She'll wait until they're going to break, then say something outrageous. Try and interrupt her before she gets it out."

The assistant director said, "We'll go to break. Set you up, and then go live. Ready?"

Bright and focused lights highlighted Hartman's sleek desk set before an LED wall. Two operators positioned cameras on the sides of the stage. A fourth camera was on a mechanical boom.

Deirdre sat in the guest chair, and the assistant director quickly attached a microphone to her blouse. "Give me a test. Say something."

"Hello," Deirdre said.

"Louder."

"Hello." She forced the word through her constricted throat.

"There's water if you need it," the AD said and hurried off the stage.

Deirdre mentally reviewed the points she needed to make. Allan Hansen is a champion of individual rights. Appeal to the Libertarians. If we don't elect him, this country is doomed. He's the lone patriot standing between us and the passage of the Sentinel Act. No! Stay on message. Maybe she had gotten too close to the candidate. She was thinking like him now, not for him.

Hartman was hunched over notes, his lips moving in a silent rehearsal. The leather-clad Regina stared at the camera as if it was Snow White's mirror. Her straightened hair was held in place with a polyurethane sheen.

Deirdre looked around for the director she was supposed to keep her eye on. Was it the AD wearing the headset closing the fingers of her open hand and mouthing the descending seconds?

Deirdre watched Regina smile seductively toward the center camera.

None of the cameras had a red light on. Which would be the first camera she was supposed to look into? The stage that had seemed so cold when she arrived was now desert hot.

The AD's hand closed to a fist. The light on the right-side camera came on. Hartman was speaking to it. Regina continued to look into the central camera. That was the one that would come on to shoot her. Deirdre imitated Regina's focus.

"We are now joined by well-known political commentator Mary Regina and Deirdre Owens, campaign manager for Allan Hansen, incumbent candidate for the US Senate from California. Deirdre Owens was one of the last persons to see Jacob Gillium alive. Who was Jacob Gillium? For those of you who have not been following this story . . ." Hartman presented the opposition's case from Berkeley to the shooting of Gillium as if proven, indisputable fact. Then, his focus narrowed on her. "Deirdre Owens, is Senator Hansen a terrorist sympathizer? Or, as some are saying, a terrorist himself?"

The red light in the center camera came on. Deirdre stared into the all-seeing round eye. Blood rushed into her head. *Imagine you're talking to someone you know*, Metcalf had coached her. It's a hot medium. Be cool, simple.

"No," Deirdre said with a nearly emotionless, flat tone.

On-air silence is exaggerated. They gave her what seemed like a millisecond to continue if she had something to say before Regina seized the stage.

"Of course he is. Allan Ali Hansen," –she pronounced the name like *Muhammad Ali*, making Hansen sound like he had just come down from the mountains of Afghanistan to murder Americans–"has been a radical since his Berserkly days when he and Lauren Bastini, the prime suspect in the recent attack on Washington, conspired to plant bombs. They were anarchists then and Ali Hansen is an anarchist now. The man hates America!"

The right camera light came on. Hartman smiled at Regina like she was his precocious child. "How could a US senator be a terrorist? Where's your proof?"

Regina turned to the left camera, anticipating the shot. "It's in the FBI records. He was put on trial and convicted of conspiring against the United States. He was never brought to justice because he agreed to turn state's evidence. Ali Hansen copped a plea. How long are we going to let him get away with this? Are we going to wait until he and his terrorist cell succeed in a disastrous terrorist attack on the United States? This man is a terrorist bent on the destruction of the United States of America."

*Say something! Don't just sit there*, Deirdre screamed at herself, but she felt lost in a fog.

The red light came on the center camera. Deirdre managed a closed-mouth smile. She felt like she had when her father criticized her. She was weak and submissive. She stared at the camera lens, impotent before the whole world.

Hartman jumped in, egging Regina on. "How could Senator Hansen hide a charge like that on his record? Why hasn't this come out?"

Regina spoke to the center camera. "Because Ali Hansen is a darling of the liberal press. *They* think a terrorist should have the right to bomb us." Regina leaned forward and narrowed her eyes. "Are we insane? Wake up, people. This isn't a game. Having Ali Hansen in the United States Senate is a threat to all our security."

"Why haven't we heard of the conviction before?" Hartman asked with a faint effort to appear impartial.

"The FBI has the files. On behalf of all Americans who want safety in our homes and communities and will defend the lives of our children, family, and businesses, I demand that the FBI release all information that it has regarding Ali Hansen's involvement in . . ."

"His name is Allan, Allan Hansen." Deirdre's voice was firm.

The left camera blinked on. Deirdre stared into the lens. "Allan Hansen risked his life to infiltrate a dangerous radical group at the University of California. He helped prevent a terrorist incident."

"Then why won't he release his FBI file?" Regina tried to reclaim the camera.

The left camera blinked off but came back on when Deirdre continued, "And he is working today in the United States Senate to protect you from those who would steal your liberty in the name of national security, would encourage neighbor to spy on neighbor, US citizens to be held in indefinite detention, their constitutional rights suspended, their homes and records searched without court approval."

She was saying what Hansen wanted her to say. She was the candidate now.

Hartman grinned quickly but then looked deadly serious when the right camera blinked on. "The Sentinel Act, which Senator Hansen," he emphasized the name, "is opposed to, would help law enforcement track sex offenders. Every major national security organization is asking for the passage of this act. Sex traffickers are licking their chops because they have a US senator in their camp."

Sweat broke through the stage makeup. Deirdre swallowed hard and forced words through her constricted throat, trying to keep her voice from trembling.

"Next week, the Senate will take up the Sentinel Act. Senator Hansen and the other members of the Judiciary Committee . . ."

Regina interrupted, "Senator Hansen and the radical left will take the security of this country back to the days before 9/11. We have just experienced how vulnerable we are to terrorist attacks from one of Hansen's coconspirators. We have to protect ourselves. The Surrender Act is what Hansen wants. He'll hand terrorists an open invitation to attack us."

Deirdre continued, "The Sentinel Act will . . ."

Hartman cut her off. "Is Allan Hansen a radical? Like when he was a student at Berkeley?"

The way he said *Berkeley* wasn't a silent dog whistle–it was a shift change whistle at the auto plant in Irvine, to the farmer working his combine in the Central Valley, a Mendocino racist holding on to her last hope of white privilege.

Deirdre had the timing. She barely let Hartman finish his question before blurting, "Of course not. He's a hero. He worked with the FBI to stop a terrorist act."

Regina smiled. "If he's a hero, then let us see the records. Every Freedom of Information request has failed to turn up any evidence of Allan Hansen being this hero you describe."

"And where do they say he was anything else but a hero?"

The director held up five fingers.

"All right," Hartman said. "We'll have to see how this develops."

Deirdre remembered Metcalf's warning. Out of the corner of her eye, she saw Regina breathe deeply.

Deirdre blurted as Regina began to speak, "Why isn't the Justice Department investigating election interference and evidence tampering by FBI Special Agent George Blum?"

"Ali Hansen . . ."Regina tried to recover, but all the red lights were off on the cameras. Their segment was over.

The PA came on the dead set to remove the microphone from her collar and a flesh-colored earpiece.

Deirdre had no earpiece. She'd not been privy to the discussions and directions from the control booth. She was to be the innocent victim torn apart by the host and accomplice guest. Judging from Regina's pinched face, the victim had inflicted unexpected damage.

A voice spoke through an overhead speaker. "Deirdre, thank you. Michael Flemings, producer of *The EDGE*. I'd like to speak to you about coming back for a longer segment."

Deirdre looked up to the glass-fronted box over the stage at a figure who waved at her.

*OK-what the fuck*? She was in the stage light now, not where she wanted to be, but she felt a surge of power as if she'd grown, put on muscle.

Offstage, Regina was as friendly as if they'd just played a tough tennis match against each other. "You made some great points. I think Hansen's right to worry about expanding the government's surveillance powers."

Deirdre squinted and raised her palms upward as if to ask, *Are you serious? Was this all a game?*

"Great shot calling out the special agent by name. Good entertainment," Regina said. "See you soon."

# TWELVE

## COPPER GAL

Uberhoff was at the White House for his ten-thirty daily security briefing of the president. Something about the Oval Office made you feel as if you were standing on the bridge of the ship of the world. Delivering the president's security briefing each morning was the unadulterated power of the Director National Intelligence. Uberhoff was the filter on the spigot through which all the intelligence–clandestine and overt–collected from all the eighteen US government intelligence agencies–from satellites to human assets around the world–was delivered to the chief executive.

Uberhoff had found that the best way to interest the president was to present the information as a story with good and bad guys who wanted to hurt him. Uberhoff would know when he was losing the president's attention by the vacant stare toward a wall where a hidden flat screen was available behind sliding panels.

Uberhoff sat in a chair with padded wooden armrests and a spindled back. His briefing book rested open on the president's polished desk, named "Resolute," made from the oak timbers of the British ship HMS *Resolute* as a gift to President Rutherford B. Hayes from Queen Victoria in 1880.

"On the matter of the Blue Plains bombing, we believe that one of our prime suspects is moving. We have proof that she'd been hiding out in the West Virginia woods, but we think she's on the move."

The president's eyes focused. He rocked forward in his high-back chair and came to rest with his arms propped on the desk. "She the one that's involved with Hansen?"

"Yes, sir. From Berkeley back when the senator was in college."

"Dangerous. Think she's coming here? The White House her target?"

"Possibly. The Secret Service has been briefed."

The president scowled and shifted his weight in his chair, "I want you to find that Berkeley girl." His gaze shot to his chief of staff. "Put more resources into it. I've got a bad feeling about her."

<hr />

Ameri Battlestone walked across the cobblestone plaza on the east face of the Capitol building.

Beneath him was the visitors center and bomb shelter for the Congress, Senate, and the Supreme Court. There wasn't room for all the people who worked on the Hill. Was it first come, first serve? Was there a limit, and then the doors were closed? What about staff, the press, or visitors to the Capitol? Where were they supposed to shelter?

He'd first worked in Washington as a Supreme Court clerk, an extremely competitive and distinguished position that had identified him as one of the top young lawyers in the country.

This had been a peaceful grass and magnolia-graced park. That changed when a hijacked commercial jet was stopped from crashing into the US Capitol only by the bravery of the passengers, who instead crashed the jet into a field in Pennsylvania. Politicians, judges, and staff had run into the street with nowhere to hide or shelter.

Now the area was as much a defensible space as could be created, with two major city streets running between the Capitol and congressional office buildings. Guarded entrances, pop up anti-tank barriers in the ground, and a large police force had not stopped a mob seeking to overturn an election.

Battlestone understood the forces that motivated the evisceration of personal liberties. The freedoms he had temporarily joined Hansen's staff to defend were weaknesses. When every person could be a potential assassin, you had to know as much as possible about who shared this city and country with you. Who was a terrorist, anarchist, or radical?

He passed security at the Supreme Court building and climbed a marble staircase whose surface had been molded into undulations by decades of passing feet.

He was warmly greeted by the elderly Justice Jefferies, whose frail and small-framed body belied the vitality of his intellect. The grip from his veined and contoured hand was strong. "Welcome back, son. It's good to see you again."

They sat at a long table where Justice Jefferies would meet with his clerks on workday mornings to discuss the cases before the court. The clerks would ask questions, discuss previous rulings, and help prepare drafts of opinions or writs of certiorari to order lower courts to send up cases for review. These morning sessions were some of the most fascinating conversations in which Ameri had ever participated. The talks often ranged into details of US history and jurisprudence that could be as minute as the symbolism of the torch in the Statue of Liberty (one had to perceive liberty to obtain it) or as momentous as the strict constructionist view of the Constitution that led to the infamous 1857 Dred Scott decision denying that the Declaration of Independence applied to slaves because they were "beings of an inferior order."

Understanding that Jefferies's time was limited, Battlestone responded to the justice's question about his personal life by smiling and saying, "Fine, fine. Couldn't be better. I enjoy my work very much and often feel it is of some use. I've come to discuss the Sentinel Act. The Senate will bring it up tomorrow."

Jefferies's dark irises twinkled on his lined face. "You have come to oppose passage of this act."

Battlestone leaned back in his chair and crossed his long legs. "Absolutely. Even in this form, it represents a critical diminution by the legislature of its power and a vital infringement on civil liberties, a victory of fear over the courage to live in a democracy."

Jefferies smiled and said in a gravelly voice, "One always knew where you stood on a point, Ameri. If I may paraphrase the poet James Lowell, democracy gives every man the right to be his own oppressor."

Battlestone shook his head. "I worry that people believe these freedoms can never be taken from them and, once forsaken, can be reclaimed in an age where they feel safer."

Jefferies smiled at him kindly. "Not so long as it has vigilant citizens such as you, sir."

Battlestone's brown skin darkened as he flushed at the praise.

The justice shrugged his frail shoulders. "I too share your concern. Once lost, these freedoms will not be easily regained. We no longer live in a time when the Alien and Sedition Acts can be considered a growing pain of democracy. The power to collect and maintain information and to use it to control citizens increases by the second. However, I refuse to be pessimistic about the vigor with which our fellow citizens defend their freedoms. Never have so many been so well informed."

"And well armed," Battlestone interjected. "The invasion of our privacy by the government has all but destroyed the expectation of privacy. Who will defend the Bill of Rights?"

"I believe this court, even with its present makeup, will eventually support the Constitution. However, there are legitimate questions of the need to enforce our laws and the police powers of the state."

"They will need cloture," Battlestone said, referring to the sixty votes needed to pass the bill. With a one-vote majority, at least nine senators would have to vote against their party. "I have come to Washington at the request of Senator Hansen to provide counsel to his effort to defeat the Sentinel Act."

The justice sat back and smiled, his hands resting atop a small paunch. "You are not concerned about this last attack on Washington? I twisted my ankle, running for the shelter. You are right, Ameri, it is our fear which will lead us into tyranny. But now . . ." He arthritically rose from his chair. "I have some young clerks who—like you once were—are waiting to educate me. Would you care to sit in? I am sure they would profit from your counsel."

"Thank you, but no. I must prepare for the debate, and if it is a sham, I shall see my fears put in the public record."

Jefferies took a step with Battlestone toward the door. "I am pleased with your work, Ameri. You've done well."

"Thank you, Justice Jefferies." On an impulse, Battlestone turned and hugged the tiny man, an unimaginable gesture when he'd been his clerk. Jefferies felt fragile in his grasp.

"Come see me soon, Ameri." Jefferies patted him on the back.

Battlestone's head was lowered as he marched down the line of marble columns in the central hall. The justice was like a favorite uncle you fear will soon be gone. What then? The judiciary was resplendent with judges who'd been appointed because of their political views, judges without the character to stand for rights when in conflict with those who'd appointed them. Not hard to imagine a justice being appointed to take Jefferies's spot who would uphold the power of the state over the individual, no matter how intrusive.

Outside, the white dome of the Capitol in front of him reflected the bright summer light. When he'd been a young man, the Supreme Court had seemed like a guardian of liberty above the fray of politics. Now the nine most powerful men and women in the United States, with their life-time appointments, had become, he feared, another super-legislative body voting on party lines, not on the judicial merits of an issue. He doubted that in its present composition, the court would overturn even the most egregious violations of the Constitution contained in the legislation. And only Allan Hansen stood in the way of its passage.

———※———

Time to launch phase two of the war on those who would violate Mother Nature. Her first attack had been a shot across the bow—more a yippie statement than Weather Underground—a warning, a taunt—come and get me if you can. Now, it was time to inflict some serious damage.

143

Bastini exited her cave Wednesday, thirteen days after launching the missile at the Blue Plains treatment facility. To avoid being detected by satellite or airborne heat sensors, she emerged at two thirty in the afternoon when the temperature was in the mid-eighties and humidity equal or higher. Dressed in army surplus jungle camouflage, she hurried beneath oak and hickory trees wrapped by poison ivy and greenbrier vines.

If the law were on her trail, they would have shot her by now. They would not try to follow her. Still, she cautiously checked the twigs and piles of rocks she'd placed around her camouflaged truck, looking for signs of disturbance. With a jerk, she removed the netting with strips of green fabric used to disguise field artillery and tanks.

Inside the cab, she pulled off her floppy field hat and spread flesh-colored makeup base on her dirty face and scars. She'd been planning this escape for years. The truck was unregistered. The inspection decal on the license plate was forged with paper and adhesive tape. She pulled on a gray wig. Up close, she looked like a Halloween ghoul, but hopefully, from passing cars, she'd be taken for an old, nonthreatening lady. Nothing about her would stand much scrutiny. All she needed was a little luck and care not to commit any foolish traffic violations.

She stank and itched, but a shower waited at her destination. Only bad luck could stop her now.

Bastini reached the Capital Beltway during rush hour. Hoping for safety in numbers, she kept her wigged head low—a little old lady hunched over the steering wheel. You could only go so far in the modern surveillance state without being spotted. Every sign over the freeway had a camera. Any car could be carrying undercover police or FBI.

The traffic crept along, tailpipe to grill, on the Woodrow Wilson Bridge. Southeast of Upper Marlboro, the speed picked up. School was out, and the Chesapeake Bay was full of tourists and summer residents.

The sun was still an hour from setting when she pulled onto a dirt road running through a cornfield high with green stalks. She parked in a weathered wooden shed beside a cottage surrounded by an uncut lawn.

Asters and black-eyed Susans bloomed in beds along the brick walk up to the two cement steps, evidence of the time she'd spent there before going into hiding.

The living room was furnished with a sofa and two stuffed chairs. A framed photo of herself laughing and holding her side as a little girl—red hair aflame in the Maryland sun—between her grandparents, a memory of a distant summer, was set among others on a mantle.

She did not open the windows behind the lace curtains and pulled-down shades. She figured the FBI had been here and had probably left bugs and alarms to alert them if she returned. She headed straight for the shower, not caring that the hot water heater was off.

The cold took some getting used to, but after her ten days in the cave, the water felt good on her skin, and she stayed under for a long while, soaping herself and rinsing off twice. She avoided the mirror and its reflection of the gnarled purple burn scars on her cheek and neck, avoided looking at her flat carved-up chest, which she covered with a T-shirt before stepping into her bathing suit bottom. She took out a blue denim shirt from a bedroom closet displaying a patch that read *DOMINION*. Taped to the bottom of a dresser drawer was an ID card from the Cove Point Liquified Natural Gas facility five miles up the coast. She slipped the card into a plastic sheath and clipped it onto the breast pocket of the shirt.

The attack on Blue Plains had been a crime of opportunity presenting itself when she'd come into possession of the RPG. She'd been planning to blow up Cove Point since she'd worked on the plant's conversion from importing to exporting liquified natural gas.

Poisoned water, air, habitat, and earthquakes–the chemical extraction of the gas from shale rock was a smorgasbord of environmental destruction.

The ID was old and would not pass close inspection, but neither would she, and she didn't plan to enter through the front gate.

In a rear room that still smelled of her grandfather's Labradors, she picked up an air tank and regulator and carried it down the slope through the bluestem and sedge to the river. Papa Dave's old skipjack, once a working oyster boat, floated on the high tide. Mosquitoes hummed around her. A perch broke through the placid surface. A great blue heron gave Bastini an apprehensive look from its one-legged perch on the opposite shore.

Sloop-rigged with a sharply raked mast, a bowsprit extended out over the bow to hold the jib. A hand-carved and hand-painted trail board extended on each side of the bow with two jumping goldfish and the name *Copper Gal* after Papa Dave's nickname for her. With the centerboard raised, the wide beam floated easily to the side of the dock. She loaded the scuba gear and two weapons-filled duffle bags retrieved from the back of the truck and cast off.

The mast carved from a single two-hundred-year-old heart pine held a mainsail that extended nearly the forty-five-foot length of the boat. The canvas fluttered in the indifferent breeze as the outgoing tide floated her past old tobacco farms and drying sheds on the river.

When the sun set and she cleared the narrows, the wind picked up, and she tacked out into the bay heading north, past the lights of a planned community of "estates" and the darkness of fields bordering the brightly lit terminal and processing plant. When the shore was dark again, she turned past the wind, leeward to the Calvert Cliffs, where once she'd hunted for prehistoric shark teeth with her grandfather.

The centerboard came up and rested in its catch. She dropped the anchor just beyond the slow waves and lowered the mainsail. She had a tight schedule.

She pulled on a pair of blue jeans and slipped into the work shirt with the ID badge attached, wading to shore with her boots, hard hat, and red lunch pail in hand–looking like a worker arriving via an unusual route.

The chalky cliffs ended at a stream. The moon hadn't risen, but the facility's lights were so bright they cast a reflective glow illuminating a fence running along the banks of the operational area of the plant. She worked her way up the stream until she came to where erosion had opened a space beneath the wire bottom of the barrier.

She slid beneath the fence and was in. The Cove Point LNG facility had been built to import gas. Now, after the fracking boom, the same system worked in reverse, from heating to freezing.

Bastini didn't head for the more heavily guarded piers where the frozen gas was loaded. She worked her way through the pine forest to the processing unit, where impurities were removed from the natural gas. Then past the liquefaction units where the gas was cooled to minus 260 degrees Fahrenheit. In the open, down the road, she walked toward two rows of wheel-shaped cryogenic storage tanks.

A truck slowed as it passed her. A man in a hard hat looked at her out the driver's side. She nodded at him. He stared at her, nodded back, and drove off.

During the conversion process, she'd worked at the plant on a catering truck. She'd been friendly with the workers at the plant and learned about the operation. One had told her that he was on a maintenance crew. When the plant was operational, a storage tank was inspected every day before the arrival of an LNG tanker.

She was counting on the bureaucracy not changing routines.

A sign read: *SAFETY IS OUR BUSINESS*. Another: *LOOK! WATCH! LISTEN! SECURITY STARTS WITH YOU!* Above a lit phone on a post was another sign: *EMERGENCY*.

She turned along a line of pipes running from the storage tanks to the dock for loading on tankers. This part of the facility was brilliantly lit. She would be in full view of the security monitoring screens in the control tower beside the quay. One hesitation or misstep would give her away. *Act like you know what you're doing*, she told herself.

She approached a storage tank with two work trucks parked along a ten-foot-high fence topped with razor wire. A gate was open for the crew to conduct a safety inspection.

The bomb in her lunch bucket was not a large charge. All she wanted to do was prick the stainless steel shell that held the gas in the right spot at the right time. She had to be precise about where she placed the explosives, high enough to carry across the pipes and pumping stations that separated the tank from the dock. The tank would be filled by dawn when the tanker would arrive.

She ducked inside the steel door and listened to the sounds of the crew on the other side of the interior door, checking for leaks or corrosion.

Stairs climbed to the second floor, where she took the bomb from the lunch pail. A door led to scaffolding on the exterior part of the tank. Outside, she moved along a catwalk. This part of her plan depended on pure luck. She'd be caught if security was monitoring the screen and noticed a lone worker on the outside of the tank carrying a small object in her hand. She strode to a point facing where the ship would be docked ten hours later.

The plastique was in a cellphone with magnets glued to the back. She could not risk hiding the C-4 behind a girder. Her plot required an unimpeded shot.

On tiptoes, she placed the bomb on the steel exterior of the tank where the liquid gas would be stored.

Now all she had to do was escape and be able to detonate it at the right time.

She hurried down the internal stairs and had just reached the door when a voice behind her said, "Hey!"

She stiffened against the tremble that ran up from her legs. She would be recognized if it was someone with whom she'd worked. She could not hide her scars. She stopped, turned, and smiled, swallowed hard. "Oh, there you are," she said. "Craig Masterson sent me over. Wanted me to tell you to check the R-13 valve. It's sticking."

A man from the cleaning crew looked perplexed.

Craig Masterson was a foreman she'd gotten to know when she'd worked the food truck during the retrofit on the plant. He'd retired before she'd been fired when they discovered her fake ID.

"Also, do a communication check. He couldn't raise you."

The man reached for the walkie-talkie in a holster on his belt.

"Got to go," she said. "You got the message?"

"Yeah," he nodded, holding the communication device in his hand.

She strode out the door, retracing her steps, walking faster, forcing herself not to break into a run, expecting to hear alarms, the sound of running feet, and a shouted challenge.

If she was working here, where would she be going? She walked around to the cab of a parked truck, started to open the driver's door, and then, as if she'd forgotten something, walked back toward the woods, ducked behind a pumping station, and took a path through the pipes. The woods were just ahead. She only had a hundred yards. *Don't run, act like you're doing something, looking for something,* she told herself.

Blood pounded in her ears. She had to force air into her constricted lungs. She turned around, looked to see if anyone was coming, and ducked into the relative shade of the pine branches.

Even if she escaped, she doubted her plan would work now. Security would check the tank from top to bottom. They'd find the bomb. A helicopter swept over the dock, and a beam of light from its belly illuminated the beach. They'd find the boat before she could ever reach it. The coast guard would be on the way. Maybe she should head up the stream and try to escape overland. Maybe she should call the cellphone to explode the bomb. At least take the storage tank with her. No, stick to the plan. What did she have to lose? They still had to catch her, and she wasn't going alive.

She reached the stream and headed for the beach. The sound of the helicopter came from the shore. She stopped before leaving the stream bed. Her boat was still there. Nothing looked disturbed. The copter was heading up the beach. She ran low across the sand, took off her hard hat and boots, holding them with her lunch pail. She splashed and half swam to the side of the boat, pulled herself aboard, and reached for the anchor chain. The helicopter was almost above her.

She threw her hat and boots into the cabin, ripped off her work shirt, and grabbed a long rake-like oyster tong, pushing the boat back against the pull of the anchor chain. The copter slowed and hovered over her.

"This is a restricted area," a man's voice broadcast down on her. The prop wash rocked the boat back and forth. She shielded her eyes against the light beneath the copter, leaned back, and waved, holding the tongs as if she'd been raking for oysters. "Sorry," she mouthed, dropped the tongs, pulled the anchor free, and raised the mainsail.

The copter backed off but followed her until she'd sailed clear of the five-hundred-yard security zone. She put on her running lights and entered the shipping channel. They'd have sent a patrol boat after her if they'd been suspicious of her.

She tacked until the offshore breeze filled her main and headed out for a night sail.

# THIRTEEN

## STOP HER

They had center stage now. Something happened this morning, someone high up—very high up, Blum guessed—had bought into the Bastini threat. He'd been working the usual cover-your-bases operation in West Virginia, mustering what resources he could out of local law enforcement and FBI Martinsburg, when they'd been told to report back immediately.

The National Counterterrorism Center shared the same former horse field between the Dulles Toll Road and I-495. While the other intelligence agencies had limited focus areas, NCTC had the unique authorization to access both foreign and domestic intelligence.

Inside the ops center, the eastern seaboard with West Virginia in the center was projected on the main screen. Satellite feeds and highway surveillance video were being analyzed by techs at computers arrayed around the semicircular room.

Uberhoff, CIA Deputy Director of Operations Matthew Sorensen, and the reps from the other agencies were waiting for them in the glass-walled conference room adjacent to the ops theater.

"Sit down, you two," Uberhoff instructed.

Blum found it interesting that the meeting had been held up pending their arrival, additional evidence that Bastini was now being taken more seriously.

Blum moved to the open seat beside an admiral with four gold sleeve stripes on the cuff of his blue jacket. Barstow moved to the end of the table with the other junior staff.

Uberhoff put both hands palms down and gazed around the faces at the table. "The president has instructed that we focus more resources on finding Lauren Bastini."

Blum puckered his lips slightly to keep from smiling. Now he'd have the full resources of the US government to stop her.

"Tell us what you got," Uberhoff said to the senior FBI liaison at ODNI.

Krisky, a veteran bureau man with a long face and tired eyes, sat erect, speaking in a soft but urgent voice. "In the past thirty minutes, we've picked up her trail. The tracks found yesterday were fresh. We believe from a four-wheel truck."

A technician projected an image of a flatbed on the plasma screen on the wall opposite Blum.

Blum almost expected someone to groan. Millions of trucks like that were on the nation's highways every day.

"FBI highway surveillance monitors set around the woods picked this up." Krisky nodded at the tech.

The following image on the screen showed a black flatbed truck fitted with a camper shell. It was located under a bridge. Sun glinted off the tinted windshield and it was not possible to see who was inside. The following slide was enhanced to show the distorted image of what looked like an old woman driving. A few at the table expressed their doubt with frowns and shakes of their head.

"While the visual of the driver was not conclusive, we were able to get a good read on the tire type."

The next image was a split screen blown up to show the tread on the passing car and the cast from tire marks left in the woods. Even to the unpracticed eye, they seemed identical.

Blum observed some approving nods and note-taking around the table.

The visual changed to a license plate number. "We've run this tag. It's bogus. This is our suspect," Krisky confirmed.

The next image was a fuzzy but legible picture taken from a tollbooth camera.

"This was taken yesterday at 1810 hours at the Jersey entrance to the Holland Tunnel. We know the truck exited the tunnel and have not been able to identify the same vehicle transiting New York, nor have we been able to locate the vehicle or suspect in the city. The FBI has issued a high-level localized advisory for New York City. We're getting full cooperation from the mayor's office and NYPD's Counterterrorism Bureau. All our resources are being focused on the city now. New York airports, waterways, and transit systems are going to level 4 severe."

The final projections were images of Bastini taken from the surveillance camera that operatives from the Domestic Security Association had placed outside her cabin and another distorted picture from the tollbooth.

"We are conducting random searches and have distributed copies of Bastini's pictures and disguise to local law enforcement," Krisky concluded.

Uberhoff turned to Blum and raised his eyebrows as if he sensed Blum thought the theory was flawed.

"Blum," Uberhoff asked. "What are your feelings on this?"

Blum noticed the DNI had used the word *feelings* rather than *analysis*. To go against the presentation of his FBI senior was against bureau practice. Maybe if they hadn't turned him out like a bastard son, he'd be more circumspect.

Blum leaned forward and hunched his shoulders, glancing up at the pictures of Bastini when he spoke. "I think she's smart. I think she's been planning this for a while. She might be going to New York, but . . ." He hesitated. "That's been done. Her thing is the environment. I think her likely target is going to be a polluter—the bigger, the better. If she's gone north, I'd alert the refineries or corporate headquarters."

"Plenty of those in New York," Krisky said with the wry expression of a disapproving teacher.

"We have no evidence she's ever been there or scoped it out. New York might not be her target," Blum countered.

"Has the bureau developed a potential target list?" Uberhoff asked.

Krisky hesitated and looked at Blum, giving him the opening to speak for the FBI. "Based on her tendencies, we're focusing on what she'd perceive as a big polluter somewhere in the mid-Atlantic region, possibly a large petroleum or coal facility."

Uberhoff's eyes rolled, almost as if having a seizure. "We have to find her," the DNI said. "Let's get to work," he said and adjourned the meeting.

Blum followed Krisky into the command-and-control center. Desks with computer consoles were arranged in specific areas for each of the agencies. All faced a curved floor-to-ceiling bank of screens. The FBI desk unit was on the upper tier.

"We don't have a spot for you." Krisky was a detail man, everything in its place.

"Find one." Blum was through kissing up. Krisky had seen the way Uberhoff deferred to him.

The FBI liaison's tired eyes hardened for an instant. He frowned. "You may use my spot. You know the stations?"

"No. I need your help. Let's work together."

"Right. The terminal will put you into the bureau system. I'll guide you from there."

There was no warmth in his voice. The bureau did not tolerate insubordination.

With Krisky standing behind him, Blum called up the Bastini file and started to reread everything. Basic police work–retrace your suspect's footsteps. Most criminals fled to someplace familiar. The problem was Bastini was not fleeing. He'd bet the rent she was heading for another target. Where? The United States was nothing but targets for an eco-terrorist: oil terminals, refineries, coal mines, and nuclear reactors.

He'd predicted an East Coast target, but by the same logic of her going somewhere familiar, Bastini could be heading to Riverside, California, where she'd been raised.

He went into the Social Security database and searched her employment history. She'd worked for a catering company in Solomons, Calvert County, Maryland.

He highlighted *Sandy's Catering* and saw in their advertisement: *Servicing construction sites.*

That made sense—a lot of hungry customers in one place.

High-impact targets in the company's service area included the Cove Point Liquefied Natural Gas facility, Calvert Cliffs Nuclear Power Plant, and Pax River Naval Air Station.

He searched for large construction projects at these locations. Five years ago, Cove Point LNG converted from importing to exporting LNG.

If she'd worked at Cove Point, she'd know the layout of the plant. A tingle went up the back of his neck–a sure sign he was on to something. Blum swiveled his chair to where Krisky sat before a computer. "I have a strong case Bastini is going to attack the Cove Point LNG facility," Blum said.

"Let's go with it," Krisky said.

Blum found the name and email address of the facility security officer at Cove Point LNG and typed, *THIS IS A SPECIAL FBI ALERT: Wanted for questioning by the FBI, Lauren Bastini (see attached file). Formerly worked at the facility; may have special knowledge of security procedures and weaknesses. Heightened alert level advised for possible terrorist activity. Contact Agent Blum . . .*

"Issue alerts to the nuclear reactor and the air base," Krisky ordered an agent sitting in an adjacent spot.

"Where's the coast guard?" Blum asked.

The two old agents, energized by their mission, strode down the aisle to a lower tier. "Captain Randal," Krisky said. "We have a mid-Atlantic coastal alert."

"What do you need?"

Krisky looked to Blum.

"Can you check and see if there are any LNG tankers scheduled for loading at Cove Point?"

Captain Randal was a large man who looked like he'd done his share of enforcement. "There are most days. It's a regular pipeline."

Krisky spoke. "FBI believes there's an imminent terrorist threat to the Chesapeake and Washington, DC areas."

"What kind of threat?"

"LNG facility primary, Calvert Cliffs Nuclear Power Plant, and Pax River Naval Air Station," Blum said.

Randal smiled. "LNG explosions are a bit of a myth, you know. Better off going after any of the oil tankers out there. LNG's hard to light up, and those babies are double-hulled and packed with suppression equipment. She'd need an Exocet missile to do much damage. But I'll send the captain of the port an alert. We already provide a lot of cover just to make people happy. State police will be out there flying helicopter cover. I'll send them a heads-up too."

Blum could tell Randal wasn't buying the threat to the LNG. Blum still didn't have enough proof to switch the focus from New York. The picture from the Holland Tunnel could be totally bogus or a mistake. He was getting nervous, twitchy nervous. Time was running out. He could feel it.

"What's the address where she lived? Satellite might have something," Krisky said.

They moved down to Mike Tahaji from the National Reconnaissance Office. He inputted the address at Leason Cove and requested satellite images for a twenty-four-hour period. Quickly, they had a montage of images of a small house with a boat moored to a dock. The last visual before dark yesterday showed the boat had left the dock and was moving toward the bay, toward Cove Point. A late pass of the LNG facility showed a tanker moored at the dock.

"Can you find out where the boat went?" Blum asked, leaning over Tahaji's shoulder and looking at his computer screen.

"See what I can do." Tahaji typed commands.

"Mind coming over, Captain?" Blum called to Randal, sitting several stations away.

The coastie moved to his side.

Tahaji looked up at them. "Here's one sailed through the split. Let me blow it up."

He fed his computer commands until the image of the boat was large enough to see a lone sailor in a watch cap at the rudder.

"That the best you can do?" Blum asked.

"Yeah, unless we can catch it live. That was from last night, 2017 hours."

Randal studied the image. "That's a jack, all right. Can you make out the name on the back?"

"Tried. Best I can do for now. But I can . . ." Tahaji framed the image by dragging his mouse across the sailboat, " . . . tell the computer to search all passes over the bay for this image. We can go infrared too. We'll know where she went before long."

Blum turned to Randal. "Can you get your people to search for her?"

Randal frowned. "Jacks are common in the bay. There are probably sixty of them working the oyster beds right now. But I'll put out the word."

"Here we got a couple of more reads," Tahaji said, still typing commands into his computer.

"Where was she heading?"

"Up the shore northerly."

"To Cove Point."

"That's where I lost her."

"This is going hot," Blum said to Krisky.

Krisky rushed back to the FBI tier and pulled up the emergency contact number for Cove Point.

<hr />

Captain Reggie Delatore carried a Sig Sauer P226 in a hip holster with the ease of an old cop. Sun glinted on the water through the slanted, green-tinted windows of the control tower over the dock. He'd gotten alerts from the FBI before, but they'd never called him.

"Maximum alert," the FBI said.

"We're loading now."

"Discontinue. Terrorist attack imminent."

Stopping a loading now would cost a shitload of money to Williams Energy. Until he heard from his bosses, nothing was shutting down.

"Orange alert," he said into a facility-wide system.

From the walkie-talkie on his belt came the voice of the coast guard lieutenant on the dock. "I've got orders to stop loading."

"Roger that. Alert red," Delatore said into the microphone, clipped to a lapel on his shirt. Wasn't his call now. The coast guard had the authority to stop a load. "Quit load operation," he ordered.

Around him, the control panels and computer stations around the room represented every function of the plant. The control tower was filled with the activity of shutting down the loading of a vessel.

Valves turned off. Armed divers entered the water. His five-man security team armed themselves with automatic rifles.

Delatore thought about ordering the *REZNIC* to cast off but figured the vessel was safer moored to the dock, and there was still half the cargo to load. That was a lot of gas to be lit.

He called up the security logs for the past twenty-four hours.

An oyster boat had been seen at the creek mouth at 2340 last night. No name of the boat or description. Boats regularly passed the buoys marking the five-hundred-yard security zone and had to be chased away.

Delatore scrolled down through the log and scanned an entry about a radio miscommunication with a maintenance team in the primary heating unit. That was common. The tanks were hard to penetrate. Even with internal antennas, communications were often lost. The foreman had reported a garbled message, something about a man who had been retired for a year, typical fuck-up, nothing unusual.

Delatore split his attention between watching the tapes of the last twenty-four hours and monitoring the bifurcated screens playing the feeds of the live security cameras around the plant and vessel.

An unusual movement on one of the tanks caught his eye as he surveyed last night's tapes. He slowed the tape and intently watched a figure dressed in a company shirt and hard hat move along the catwalk on the side of the tower and place something on the tank. That wasn't right.

He pressed a button and spoke into a thin microphone rising from the console. "Base to mobile one."

"One," came the crisp reply.

"Investigate RG-5, upper portside, for foreign object. "Priority one. Unit two investigate possible foreign object on upper front RG-5. I'll guide you when I have you in sight."

"Roger."

Delatore restarted the tape and watched the figure emerge from the gate to the tank and walk across the yard to a truck. From the shape and size, he judged it to be a small man or woman. The figure started to get into the truck and then ducked around out of range of the camera.

He switched to recordings of the camera monitoring the pipelines and waited impatiently for the tape to speed to the correct time. On the live screen, two uniformed security personnel emerged from a patrol car in front of storage tank five. The temperature inside the tank would be minus 260 degrees Fahrenheit. The outer surface temperature of the tank might be around minus 10 to minus 20 degrees.

"Unit one on scene. What do you want us to do?"

"Can you climb the outside? I need you to go near the mid-level door."

"Give it a try."

The man unlocked the security gate.

"Careful," Delatore said. "Wear your gloves."

One of the men went to the external stairs and leaned his head over his shoulder where his microphone was attached. "Not too bad," he said.

"Climb to mid-level."

"Roger."

The noon sun was blazing. Bastini raked through the bottom mud in the *up'ards* shoal, feeling the unmistakable resistance of shells.

In the shipping lanes, tankers and cargo ships were moving up and down the waterways carrying their mountains of crap for the avaricious and insatiable appetites of the corrupt, stupid, and fat. She pulled the wooden rake through the muck so hard that her hands hurt. With each stroke, she called out her hatred for the industrial state.

*Profit over all, oil over health, greed, corruption. For the trees, birds, monoculture-devoured land, the poor breathing polluted air, drinking poisoned water. This is for you, Jimmy.*

She couldn't kill the beast, but she promised herself that today she would stick it in the eye.

Fat wet gunnysacks stuffed with oysters lay by the wheelhouse. Nobody would doubt she was a genuine *bayman*, as they would say on the island. She sailed west, back to the mainland.

---

In the ops center, the view of the Cove Point LNG facility was on the main screen. The image was being picked up by one of the old CORONAs, a relic of the Cold War that now lazily circled the globe watching shipping lanes, not a priority, not one of the modern IMINTs flying over hot spots that could read the numbers off a license plate.

Blum and Captain Randal stood on the lower tier behind where Sorensen and Tahaji from satellite reconnaissance sat at computer consoles. Representatives from the other eighteen agencies stood by their stations like athletes ready to be called into the game.

"Looks like a skip laying to offshore," Randal said.

"Can you give us a closer shot?" Blum asked.

Tahaji's fingers tapped on the keyboard, but it was like trying to see what was happening on the street below the Empire State Building. It was hard to tell if there was a person or piece of equipment on the rail of the boat.

"Get someone out there," Blum said.

Randal was already speaking to St. Inigoes Coast Guard Station through a phone attached to the control panel. "Investigate skipjack approximately half a nautical mile off main loading dock Cove Point."

The reaction was impressive. Within a minute, from the satellite's perspective, a US Coast Guard fast-response patrol boat with a Browning M2HB .50-caliber machine gun on the bow could be seen moving from the perimeter patrol around Cove Point toward the skipjack. On the screen, a helicopter appeared as a mosquito-sized shape moving across the water.

"Is that a frogman?" Blum bent over and strained to see the tiny figure.

"We got underwater security around the vessel," Randal said. "They won't get in that way."

Maybe Bastini was not on this boat. Blum searched the surrounding water for another threat. "Hold back some of your protection," he said over his shoulder.

"They know what they're doing," the coast guard captain said tersely.

Blum ignored the buzz of his cellphone receiving a message. He guessed how Lauren Bastini planned to attack Cove Point. She was too far out to be doing anything else. "She's got a cellphone trigger." Blum opened his cellphone and redialed the number to Cove Point security. The number rang once, and then Blum's hand dropped.

On the screen, a bright line of light seemed to shoot out of the side of storage tank 5 and hit the vessel midship. It was as if someone had a ray gun aimed at the *REZNIC*.

The seventy-five-thousand-ton vessel rolled toward the bay. The beam of fire appeared to pass through the hull, expanding as it rolled over the water. Then, the *REZNIC* exploded with a light so bright it obscured the initial blast. Eruptions of gas tanks on the shore burst like the synchronized flashes of a fireworks show.

The wave of destruction expanded in a circle from beneath a fiery cloud across the water and facility. Flickers identified schools, houses, and stores in the surrounding communities igniting. On the water, the patrol boats and the skipjack that had attracted their attention disappeared into the boiling flaming wall.

Blum stared at the large screen. This was his fault. From beginning to end, he was to blame. He'd known who was going to do this, knew where to find her, and he had failed to stop her.

"Oh God, it's going to hit Calvert Cliffs Nuclear Power Plant," Randal said.

Blum diverted his attention from the water to where the edge of the destruction was spreading like a hurricane wall up the shore.

Krisky lifted a red phone from the console. "Priority level 1, mid-Atlantic US."

All over the world, no matter where they were, military, government, and political leaders and their security details from the president to the director of national intelligence were receiving the message Sorensen was typing into his computer.

*LNG blast Cove Point, massive destruction, possible nuclear effect Calvert Cliffs NPP.*

"Missy, what do you have?" Krisky called to the liaison with the Department of Energy.

Missy Compton, a small woman with the wiry body of a runner, rapidly tapped her password into the DOE website and entered the department's emergency response center.

"I'm going into the plant's operational read," she said over her shoulder.

The screen was filled with windows of fluctuating graphs, dials, and charts. It was illegible to Blum. Compton appeared to read and digest the information instantly.

"There's a problem in the spent fuel containment block–a graphite fire. They're losing coolant. Backup systems are not responding. Something is interfering with the controls. They're issuing a general emergency alert. The sirens are going off."

Blum stared at fire and smoke clearing on the main screen. Flaming boats and ships lay ruined across the Chesapeake like candles on a blue cake. They had to get Bastini. She had an escape plan. She was not a suicide bomber. But they could not order men into an area that might be radioactive.

The young lawyer, Barstow, was at Blum's side. "Shouldn't we notify the director?" he asked softly, as if giving him a clue.

For an instant, Blum couldn't sort which director Barstow was talking about–the FBI director or the director of national intelligence?

He looked at his cellphone and saw the message he'd received the moment before the attack on Cove Point.

*38.3862346° N, -76.4191171° W*

---

The Calvert Cliffs Nuclear Power Plant, fifty-one miles southeast of Washington, stored spent fuel assemblies in water-filled pools to allow for cooling and decay of gamma and neutron radiation.

The crew working on the switch box that housed the electrical control cables regulating the flow of water only had one breath before their lungs burned as the superheated air from Cove Point swept over them. The insulation around the cables burned through the housing, igniting the polyurethane seals into the containment area. The heat poured through the breach, evaporating the water in the pool, causing a radioactive cloud to escape through the open conduits into the outside air.

Operators inside the main facility were dealing with multiple fires and destroyed controls. They'd been spared the same incineration as their fellow workers by the concrete walls and self-contained breathing system. Automatic sprinklers and fire-suppression devices were going off all over the plant.

In the confusion, they didn't notice that the spent fuel storage unit had been breached until sensors detected a radioactive cloud rising from the facility blowing northeast toward Washington, DC.

---

Deirdre sat beside Ameri Battlestone in the visitors gallery perched over the small amphitheater of the Senate floor. Hansen had asked Battlestone to help prepare his arguments against the Sentinel Act.

The gallery was packed with citizens who wanted increased protection and those who wanted to protect their privacy from the government.

Hansen's unamplified voice rose passionately as he spoke words crafted by Battlestone.

"The people trust their present leaders, who may well show the respect of liberty owed to a free people. But what of those leaders who are to come? Those who choose not to govern but to rule!"

Hansen's voice rose to a theatrical emphasis as he leaned across the desk.

Deirdre saw uniformed capitol police rushing in from the exits. Something was wrong.

A sergeant at arms in a blue jacket stepped to the dais and spoke to the junior senator seated in the president's chair. The senator's face blanched. He stood as if ready to break into a run, banged the ivory gavel against the desk, and called, "Will the senator suspend for a moment?"

Absorbed in his oration, Hansen appeared to be the last to notice the disturbance spreading throughout the chamber. Caught in mid-breath, he looked at the chair suspiciously. "Yes?"

"We must evacuate. They believe the threat is nuclear. Senators will follow evacuation procedures," the president pro tempore called as he hurried for the exit with a Capitol Hill police officer at his elbow to guide and protect him.

Hansen's hand dropped, and his head hung. He looked defeated. "I suggest the absence of a quorum." His voice was barely a whisper.

Other sergeants at arms came to his side.

A choking fear gripped Deirdre's chest. Battlestone stayed at her side with his hand near her elbow as if ready to push her through the stream of evacuees trying to escape. To where—where could you go to escape a nuclear attack? Was it a missile? A dirty bomb?

Bells rang.

Outside the gallery, the hallway was filled with staffers, tourists, and lobbyists. Capitol Hill police pushed through the swarm without a purpose other than to join the escape.

"Watch where you're going!" an older woman snapped at a man who had bumped into her, holding her shoulders back, walking casually as if dignity was more important than survival.

Thirty people pressed in around the elevators. She followed the flow to the stairs. A fat man in a shiny tight-weave suit pushed roughly past her.

The closer to the exit, the denser the mass trying to escape, pressing behind like a stampede that would trample her if she faltered. The flow met and pooled at stairs that led to the floor of the Senate. Deirdre stepped back into a recess framing a marble bust of some long-dead senator. She'd lost contact with Battlestone.

"Senators only! Senators only!" A policewoman protected an elevator.

People were leaning into Deirdre, pushing her back into the packed nook. It was like being trapped in an overcrowded New York subway.

"Any idea what's going on?" An intense-looking young man with round tortoiseshell glasses squeezed into Deirdre's sanctuary.

She shook her head.

A man whose back pressed against Deirdre's breasts said, "Don't know, my phone's down." He kept his focus on the miniature screen.

"Yeah, mine too."

"Nuclear attack," someone, maybe three bodies away, said.

"Damn! What can we do here? Can they seal this off?"

The man with the cellphone leaned farther into Deirdre so she could feel the bulge of his wallet against her thigh.

"I don't think so," a man said from somewhere behind her.

Where was Ameri Battlestone? She saw Joe Upton try to move through the herd with a swimming motion as if the people in his path were a fluid to be moved aside.

A woman with crooked teeth shrugged her narrow shoulders. "I don't know where to go. Might as well stay here?" The statement was more of a question.

Deirdre didn't know where else to go either.

A woman pressing against Deirdre's shoulder held her hands together and prayed softly under her breath.

"Lord, make me an instrument of your peace."

She thought of her father. He'd been fatalistic about death . . .*When it's my time.* His time had come on his tractor from a heart attack because he'd not wanted to spend the money or waste the time to go see a doctor when he'd had chest pains. Was she about to join him?

She saw Hansen, tall in the mass. Two burly sergeants at arms were at his side, clearing a path for him. "Allan," she called and tried to move toward him.

He saw her and struggled to reach her. "Come with me." He took her hand and, with the help of the sergeants-at-arms, pushed back through the crowd toward the Senate floor.

Deirdre realized he'd come looking for her. Where was he taking her? Were there fallout shelters? She wanted to get underground, deep underground.

Hansen led her to the elevator lit with the sign: *Senators Only.*

"She's with me," Hansen said to one of the blue coats.

"Follow me please, Senator," a police officer said.

An officer operated the elevator that dropped them into the Capitol sub-basement. Another was waiting to rush them into a tunnel that led to a guarded door.

"Senators and senior staff only. Have your IDs out."

"She's on my staff," Hansen said, escorting her past the throng at the door.

The adrenaline of flight pumped breaths into gasps. She was being saved. Hansen was saving her while Battlestone and thousands, maybe millions, would die. How long would they have to stay underground?

Images of a post-holocaust world, Washington in ruins, mutant survivors picking through the wasteland, passed through her thoughts.

They descended on a gradually sloping walkway to another guarded entrance that looked like a bank vault door. Nobody tried to stop Deirdre this time, and she followed Hansen into an open room where Supreme Court justices, senators, congresspeople, and senior staff gathered, asking each other questions about what had happened. Deirdre overheard a senior senator say that a dirty bomb had gone off at Reagan Airport.

Hansen did not stop to exchange gossip but passed through the mezzanine into an auditorium set up like a college lecture hall with descending rows of first-class airline sleeper chairs equipped with computers and screens facing a stage.

"We get to bring in one staff person," Hansen said.

She looked up at him and saw a teacher. She believed and trusted in his love for her. "Thanks for choosing me." She hugged herself to stop shaking.

While other cellphones were down, the senators appeared to have their own system that allowed them to reach outside the bunker.

"I'm safe. We don't know what happened exactly. It appears to be local. Glad you're in Aspen." Deirdre heard him say.

A pang of jealousy cut through Deirdre's fear. She didn't want to listen to Hansen talk to his wife.

Hansen had married the wealthy divorcee when he was already a senator. She appeared to like the social aspect of being a senator's wife but not the grind of a campaign. She was barely a presence in his life, from Deirdre's perspective. Maybe Deirdre kept it that way to feel better about sleeping with him.

She walked down the row of senators as if moving through a movie theater built to preserve and keep functioning the legislative and judicial branches of government in case of an attack on the Capitol.

There was the hollow preparatory sound of a microphone being turned on. Senate Majority Leader Lyons addressed the assemblage. "Ladies and gentlemen."

Deirdre stopped at the edge of the row of seats and concentrated on the courtly man at the desk on the small stage like everyone else in the underground hall.

"We've come here as a precaution." Lyon's voice carried well enough in the chamber without the amplification from speakers in the walls around the room. "I want you all to know that to the best of our knowledge, there has been no direct nuclear attack on Washington. There has been an incident. Reports are that it might be terrorism at the Cove Point Liquid Natural Gas facility approximately sixty miles from here. The explosion reached a nearby nuclear facility, which has unfortunately sustained some damage. I want to assure those of you worried about your families that we do not know at this point if there is any actual danger to life and limb here in Washington. Those of you with family and friends in the blast range, I'm terribly afraid the news is dire. Our thoughts and prayers ..."

"Then why are we here?" a congressman shouted in a manner more typical of the British House of Commons than the US Congress.

"We're trying to find that out," the leader responded to the growing chorus of murmuring in the strange room. "As soon as the all clear sounds, we'll let you know."

Grumbling spread and members of Congress stood up from their seats, but Deirdre saw nobody leaving. She found her way to an anteroom off the main floor where staffers stood in small groups, greeted each other, and huddled around computer stations. She didn't recognize anyone and moved to a wall where a plasma television screen was broadcasting the news.

A female anchor was trying too hard to be authoritative and calm, so her voice sounded brittle and cracked at the edges. "Officials are urging people to remain indoors, close all doors and windows, turn off intakes. If your children are in school, do not go to them. They will be safe there. Keep pets inside. If you can, shelter farm animals. Cover food. Eat and drink from sealed containers or well water. If you must go outside, use your COVID mask to cover your nose and mouth. When back inside, take a shower. Wash your clothes. If you are in your car, proceed as soon as possible to shelter. If it is necessary, you will be provided with iodine pills to protect your thyroid gland."

How were people to get these pills if they couldn't go out? As if to reinforce the message to stay off the roads, the news broadcast went to a story about impassable traffic jams moving away from the Chesapeake Bay and closed roads leading into the area.

Deirdre looked around the bunker. Would she have to spend days, maybe weeks, here? Did they have showers? Changes of clothes? Food? It was like a bad zombie movie, trapped underground with the US Congress.

———————◆———————

Blum reached Sabah.

"The attack on Cove Point was carried out by Lauren Bastini."

"How do you know this?"

"She sent me a text, the coordinates, seconds before the attack."

"You know the text was sent by Bastini?"

"No, but I have a strong suspicion. I gave her this number when I was trying to get her to contact me." *When he'd started this calamity.*

Sabah hesitated. Blum imaged him weighing the value of Blum's suspicion.

"We'll run a trace on the number. Why didn't we know this before-hand?" Sabah asked.

"I emailed the Southern Maryland lead agent." Blum heard how lame he sounded.

"When?"

"An hour before the incident. We were looking for her in New York." His excuse sounded even more pathetic. There was no way to avoid the blame. The suspect he'd been trailing had just blown up an LNG facility and a nuclear power plant.

"I'll look into it."

"She's out on the bay. I have her coordinates."

"Bastini?"

"Yes!"

Sabah hesitated. "It's radioactive out there now. We have to send a special team."

"I highly recommend it."

"All right. I'll handle this. What is ODNI doing?"

"I'm in the Situation Room station." That wasn't an answer. They weren't doing anything but looking and waiting. "This should be an FBI operation," Blum added with a pleading tone.

"We might have to defer to NERT," Sabah said.

The National Emergency Response Team was designated to respond to an act of nuclear terrorism. "I don't think that Calvert Cliffs was her primary target. She's out in the bay. I saw her on a satellite feed. Her boat is burning. She has to be out there."

"Work through ODNI. We'll do what we can here," Sabah said and hung up on him.

Again, Blum felt the separation—neither fish nor fowl—he was caught in between, no longer part of the FBI. No longer part of Sabah's *we*. He must have had a terrifying expression based on the way Barstow held out a phone to him as if he might rip it from his hand.

"It's the director," Barstow said.

Blum took the phone. "Yes, sir?"

"I need to brief the president on this. What do you have?"

"It's Lauren Bastini. She planted a bomb at the LNG facility. She's out on the bay. We can catch her if we get someone out there."

"I want you to work with the Pentagon and DOE on this. Catch her!"

"Yes, sir." Blum hung his head. This was a law enforcement operation. What did soldiers and nuclear technicians know about catching a terrorist who'd spent years planning an attack?

He handed the phone back to the nervous young lawyer and looked at the main screen. The CORONA satellite had passed, and they had no visual of the bay.

———◦◉◦———

Ten minutes after the majority leader had made his first announcement, he returned to the stage. Deirdre moved from the plasma screen to the doorway and peered over the shoulders of staffers.

"We have been informed that the operators at Calvert Cliffs have stabilized the situation at their facility, and there is no longer a danger of radioactive release. We can return to our families and duties now. May God bless America."

There was the standard cheer at the line, and a few shouted amens. In the hubbub of laughter and relief of the crowd pressing toward the exit, Deirdre heard the words *overreaction* and *unnecessary panic*. Maybe it had been, but there wasn't much time for debate in a nuclear world.

After the auditorium had mostly cleared, Hansen remained in his seat, studying the computer screen attached to his chair. Deirdre waited while the aisle emptied, and he still did not move. Finally, he stood up and came to her. "The FBI's prime suspect is Lauren Bastini," he said, his mouth twisted into an angry scowl. "What could possibly make someone do such a thing?"

Deirdre recognized that the question was rhetorical and did not attempt an answer. She assumed the Sentinel Act would pass now. Lauren Bastini had surely single-handedly convinced the majority of the American people that their Constitution aided terrorists. Liberties had to be sacrificed to protect family and home. When one person could blow up an LNG facility and a nuclear power plant, the power of the individual became too great a threat to the collective well-being of the whole.

Deirdre wanted to get away from Washington and this constant nervous edge. It wasn't like she had weak nerves and had not seen or felt the threat of violence. Violence wasn't personal. Radioactive fallout fell on the wicked as it did the just.

She and Hansen were one of the last to leave. The senator was pensive, his eyes downcast, head lowered. They rode up in the elevator. Hansen looked down at her and said, "I'm not giving up. I'm not."

Her chest swelled, and she nodded with a slight smile. "I know," she said, proud of him.

# FOURTEEN

## HOSTAGES

Cold December rain whipped Bastini from low dense clouds and plopped onto her green plastic poncho that covered a waterproof waist pack stuffed with ammunition, timers, and plastique. The hard form of a MAC-10 bounced off her shoulder.

Her muscles and nerves twisted with pain from seventy-three days of crouching inside the narrow grotto in the West Virginia mountains. She rubbed a dirt-blacked hand through her matted hair, but the sleeting rain could not wash away the filth that clung to her. Hunching against the wind, she coughed and plodded on through the wet night.

The way out of the woods was treacherous without light. She slipped on slimy rocks and stepped into unseen pools of dark water until only the cold-induced numbness deadened the pain of her hunger, fatigue, cuts, and bruises. By the time she reached the highway, her clothes were so heavy with water and mud she made a sloshing sound with each step, like a wet rag hitting a wall. She kept her hand near the trigger ready to fight but doubted the dirty and wet gun would fire.

Unsure where she'd come out of the woods, Bastini turned up the steep incline and trudged with gasping breaths.

She'd hidden as long as she could—had strength for one more move, one blow, and then she was leaving the country. If the feds had discovered her safe house, that would be her last fight.

No cars or trucks passed her as she struggled on another mile until she reached the summit. The wind blew so furiously she had to bend forward to take each step.

Four run-down wooden houses stood beside an abandoned gas station. A sign read, *US Post Office, Lorton, West Virginia*—so cold and forlorn, even the meth heads had left.

Past an old cylindrical gas pump, up a rutted dirt driveway, she came to a dark shotgun house.

She unlocked a padlock on a detached wooden garage door with trembling hands. At the sight of the old Honda inside, she gurgled and muttered, "Good."

She went around back and climbed three steps that sagged beneath her weight. She hoisted the MAC and peered through a broken window. The house looked as deserted as when she'd found it. Nothing appeared disturbed since she'd stocked the house for her next attack on the industrial monster.

She went inside and heard rats scurrying in the walls but nothing more. If the place was bugged or she'd tripped an unseen alarm, she hoped she would hear them when they came. She stripped off her soggy clothes, wrapped herself in a sleeping bag and blanket, cradled the gun in her hand, and fell into a deep sleep.

———◦◎◦———

Blum was no longer assigned to ODNI. The higher-ups in the bureau had probably decided that an investigative procedure to fire him would call too much attention to matters they were trying to bury. He'd been sent back to the LA office to wait for his retirement. That didn't stop him from studying Bastini's history and patterns.

Her grandfather's burnt skipjack had been carefully recovered from the bottom of the bay, but not her body or the phone the FBI digital forensics team said had sent Blum the coordinates to the attack.

Until he had proof that Bastini was dead, he assumed she was alive and planning her next attack.

A break came three weeks before Christmas when a Nevada Highway Patrol dashboard camera picked up a partial visual of the driver of a passing car headed west. A possible Bastini match was made with an experimental facial-recognition program developed by the National Institute of Standards and Technology at the Department of Commerce.

The clue was enough for Blum to explore possible West Coast targets, including himself. Why had she sent him the coordinates for the Cove Point attack except to taunt him? She had reason enough to want to kill him, dating back to his undercover days as Cliffy. He was willing to hold himself out as bait if she could be flushed out.

He'd received an invitation to the annual meeting of the Domestic Security Association in Riverside at the Mission Inn. Probably payback for the fat IDIQ contract he'd thrown their way in their failed attempt to pressure Bastini.

She'd once lived at the Mission Inn when it was a run-down hippie warren—before the city had used federal redevelopment money to renovate the hotel as part of a downtown revival plan. Now an odd blend of Victorian and Craftsman influences, the hotel was a fanciful array of kitsch done up to the hilt for a Dickensian Christmas.

She might still know ways to move unseen around the hotel.

The way she'd defeated the DSA operatives attempting to follow her car was evidence that she knew who had been following her. Reason enough for her to target the DSA gala dinner.

If nothing else, the Domestic Security Association was a good connection to get some consulting work when he retired in six months.

Dressed in a blazer paired with dress pants for the dinner, he removed an FBI field kit from the trunk of his car and entered the hotel looking like a guest with a small hard suitcase.

For a half hour, he explored the complex layout of interconnected wings, a mix of architectural styles, arches, domes, spires, courtyards, and gardens. The hotel's fame and charm came from an eccentric mix of architecture–Norman castle meets Franciscan chapel. Whoever built this place was way too weird and had too much money.

Guests for the DSA gala were assembling in the Grand Parisian Ballroom beneath exposed-wood-beam ceilings for the cocktail stage of the event. Damask draperies framed stained glass windows. Carolers in long skirts, capes, bonnets, top hats, ascots, and plaid vests serenaded from a minstrel's balcony.

A feeling of impotence caused Blum to frown and his shoulders to slump. He didn't feel like socializing and was not very good at it when he did.

He was flying blind, hoping for a miracle to make up for his failures. Even if Bastini *was* here, he had no idea how to find her among the warren of rooms, holiday festivities, and guests.

He had time for another sweep before the dinner.

Carrying his field kit past the fountain on the Spanish patio, he returned to the main lobby.

Beneath a rotunda, he saw a movement that did not fit with the pattern of guests and sightseers of the hotel's over-the-top Christmas decor.

A figure dressed like Santa hurried toward the door to the street. With the place done up like a five-star Santa's village, there was nothing remarkable about a St. Nick sighting. But this was a bedraggled, downtrodden Santa who looked like he'd been in the suit for a week.

The costumed figure had emerged from a service door. Maybe Santa was a hotel employee who knew the shortcuts, like Bastini would.

Blum retraced Santa's path past a parked maid's cart into one of the hidden arteries every hotel uses to move about food, supplies, and employees. He came to a wooden door that appeared out of place in the utilitarian functioning of the passage.

A man dressed in a burnt-orange waist jacket, carrying a tray on an upturned palm, hurried past.

Blum stopped him. "Where does this go?"

"The Grand Parisian Ballroom," the Latino said.

Blum tried the door, but it was locked.

"Hey," Blum again called to the waiter's back. "You got a key?"

"No key."

The service elevator came, and the waiter started to get in.

"Wait." Blum strode toward him.

"Yes?" The waiter held the tray in one hand and the elevator door open with the other.

"You see a Santa coming through here?"

The waiter pursed his lips and squinted at Blum.

"You know," Blum held his own Santa-like belly, "Santa, ho-ho-ho."

"Ah." The man smiled. "Santa! He come out there." The waiter nodded toward the wooden door.

Elevator bells began to complain about the service door being held open. The waiter smiled apologetically as he let the doors close.

Blum hurried back to the lobby and stepped in front of a man checking in at the reception desk. He showed his blue-and-gold FBI special agent badge. "I need to speak to hotel security right away."

The uniformed clerk's eyes expanded. "Excuse me," she said to the guest and picked up a phone. "Security, front desk."

Blum waited impatiently until a man dressed in a workaday brown suit came out from the patio dining area.

"I'm Lyle Cinquist, hotel security."

"Blum, FBI. We have a situation here. Mind coming with me?" He didn't wait for an answer and led the man to the wooden door.

"What's behind there?"

Cinquist squinted as if trying to remember. "Back-of-the-house corridor to deliver food and services."

"Any idea why Santa would be coming out of there?"

Cinquist squinted again. "No."

"Mind opening it so I can see where it goes."

"No problem." Cinquist pulled a chain of keys from his belt, found the right one, and tried to put it into the lock. "Something's jamming it." He bent over and peered into the keyhole. "Somebody's stuck something in there. Looks like gum."

"Mr. Cinquist, I'm advising you to evacuate the premises."

The man's eyes closed, and he shook his head. "No way. We've got a hotel full of guests. Unless you got something solid, I can't clear them out."

Blum's phone buzzed with a message. He looked down and saw: *33.9834° N, 117.3733° W.*

He showed the phone to Cinquist. "These the coordinates for the hotel?"

Cinquist tilted his head and half smiled as if to humor a madman. "I don't know."

Blum googled: geographical coordinates for the Mission Inn.

*33.9834° N, 117.3733° W:* came up on the screen of his smartphone.

He showed the phone to Cinquist. "I'm telling you this is a warning, the same warning that was used before the Cove Point LNG disaster. We have a situation."

"And you'll take responsibility?"

Blum was already calling the Interagency Joint Terrorism Task Force. He identified himself and said, "I have a high reason to believe Lauren Bastini has planted a bomb at the Mission Inn, Riverside. I strongly advise evacuation of immediate area and dispatch of Hazardous Device team for counterterrorism response."

The desk officer at the task force repeated the threat and location with no argument or worry about guest inconvenience.

Cinquist spread his hands. "All we got is some gum in the keyhole. Any kid could have done that."

Blum didn't have time to go through his resume with the wannabe. He opened the hard case and removed what looked like a ruggedized smartphone from its foam rubber compartment, pulled out an antenna, set the frequency range to 5G networks, and set the jamming signal to maximum range.

All cellphones within a range of four hundred yards went dead. "Is there another passage to the Grand Parisian Ballroom?"

Cinquist studied him, eyes narrowed with suspicion as if wanting to believe that Blum was an impostor playing a prank on him and the hotel. "Hold on about evacuating. We don't want to start a panic."

Blum held out his hand up the hall.

Cinquist started a rapid stride. "Not at least until I see something."

Fire alarm bells began to ring throughout the hotel. JTTF had called in the alarm.

Cinquist frowned and looked back at the lobby.

"Take me to where this passage enters the ballroom. The faster we find out what's going on, the quicker this will end," Blum said.

They broke into a trot down an alleyway between two generations of the hotel onto a patio outside what looked like a Gothic chapel with a bell tower.

Alarm bells mixed with police sirens. The sound of a child crying came from the patio behind them.

The DSA executive director dressed in a tuxedo stood inside the entrance to the ballroom.

"What's going on?" he demanded.

"I believe Lauren Bastini has planted explosives here. I strongly suggest you and your guests exit the premises now," Blum said.

Branson's eyes bulged. Blum didn't need to elaborate. The DSA director grabbed his wife's hand and followed the costumed revelers out of the hotel.

Cinquist headed across the woven carpet to an archway over a service door beneath an emergency exit sign.

Cinquist fumbled for his key and was about to stick it in the hole when Blum shoved his hand away. "Wait for the bomb squad," he said, trying to remain confident, hoping he was wrong, but knowing if he was, he wouldn't even have a desk at the bureau.

---

As Bastini hurried down Main Street in Riverside, she hoped the Santa costume would work for one more night. She peered over the white beard covering her scars, saw only a few curious stares of passengers waiting for buses, and hustled off into the darkness of her old neighborhood.

When she was far enough away not to get herself blown up, she stood in the shadow of the bus station, pulled her cellphone out of her pocket, and sent Blum the coordinates. Revenge served cold. Let him think about what he could have prevented. Let him blame himself for the consequences of what he'd done to her.

She got in and turned the key to the Honda she'd driven across the country. A whirring sound preceded the motor, finally catching. It sounded like the starter going out. She might have to steal a car.

She pulled to the curb across the street of the gaudy shrine to bad taste and misplaced opulence. Mechanical figures—perfect white people in Christmas ecstasy—were arrayed on the balconies and perches amid the plethora of lights. "Merry Christmas, pigs," she seethed and dialed the cellphone attached to the detonator on the C-4 plastique explosives she planted in her Santa bag outside the door to the DSA gala.

Nothing happened. She looked at the screen of her cellphone. She wasn't getting a signal. She drove to the side of the hotel, closer to the ballroom, and tried again. Nothing. Something had gone wrong. She was tempted to go back and reset the bomb.

Alarm bells were going off. People were exiting the hotel. Sirens on emergency response vehicles were coming toward her.

Live to fight another day. If this attack had failed, another would succeed.

———◈———

Riverside Bomb Squad was a well-equipped unit. They'd obviously taken advantage of the Homeland Security money Congress had been pouring out ever since the attack on the World Trade Center.

Blum held his breath behind the portable blast screen set up on the patio. His eyes were fixed on the monitor displaying the visual of the snake being slipped beneath the door in the chapel.

"It's rigged," the officer confirmed.

The hotel had moved guests to other accommodations when the robot disabled the very nasty bomb set in a Santa's bag behind the door to the ballroom.

The plug in the keyhole had not been gum but plastique wired to a motion detector. If they had tried to jam open the door in the service corridor, it would have taken half the hotel down with it. Those not killed by the explosion would have at least been severely injured by the falling debris. The ballroom with the DSA party would have been destroyed.

The initial assessment was that the main charge was an anti-material, anti-tank submunition from a cluster bomb, most likely harvested by scavengers at the Goldwater bombing range outside of Yuma. Night and day, bombs and missiles rained down on the Chocolate Mountain and Goldwater ranges, where US and allied units trained in aerial combat. Estimates were that up to 25 percent of the bombs didn't explode. Smack up against the border with Mexico, it was as if the United States had set up an explosives bazaar where terrorists, metal scavengers, or smugglers could hunt for potent explosives. The military had gotten better at cleaning up, but there still seemed to be tons of the stuff floating around the world.

Cinquist looked at Blum with added awe. "Man, you feds sure know what you're doing."

"On a good day," Blum said softly. His deduction had come from many hours of study.

A full federal response–FBI, Homeland Security, ATF–was on the scene, leaving Blum to continue his hunt for Bastini.

He contacted FBI digital forensics and requested a trace on the source of the message on his phone. If the Sentinel Act was law, they could have had the information instantly. Now, they still needed a warrant. That would take time, and Bastini would be getting away.

Bastini couldn't have known he was so close on her trail. The latest text of coordinates had been another taunt. She was close, but where? He doubted she would give him another clue.

——◉——

Deirdre drove Hansen to his Redlands house in a rented SUV. His brother, Tommy, was in Baja, and they had the place to themselves for the night.

Since Hansen came to rescue her in the Capitol during the nuclear incident, they'd grown closer, sleeping together when they thought they could hide their affair. Deirdre felt there was more than a campaign romance.

They were listening to NPR about the attempted bombing of the Mission Inn.

Her cell rang on the speakerphone in the car. She frowned. Hansen could see Barstow's name on the display in the console. He knew about the rumors of her bondage. Better to let him hear for himself.

"What's up?" There was no affection in her voice. Why should there be?

"You know I'm working with the ODNI now."

"Why I took your call. Just heard about the Riverside incident."

"Where are you?"

She laughed. "Wouldn't you like to know?"

"You might be in trouble. The FBI thinks Lauren Bastini was the one who planted the bomb at the Mission Inn in Riverside. We think she might be coming for the senator."

"Could be."

"Do you know where the senator is? He should have protection. We've alerted the Senate sergeant at arms."

"My, my. My little boy is being bad again. Wish I was there to punish him."

"This isn't a game."

"So, you expect us to trust the FBI?"

"The senator should be protected."

"Tell him yourself. He's right here."

There was a moment of awkward silence.

"This is Allan Hansen," he said formally.

"Senator, nice to speak to you." Barstow sounded honored, then severe. "We have a strong suspicion that Lauren Bastini might have attempted a bombing in Riverside and might attempt to harm you. It is public knowledge that your official residence is in Redlands."

"Who is we?"

"I'm sorry. I'm Paul Barstow, legislative counsel with the Office of the Director of National Intelligence detailed to work on apprehending Lauren Bastini." He announced his pedigree nervously.

"Thank you for your concern, Mr. Barstow."

"Senator, really, I think …"

Deirdre interrupted his fumbling warning.

"Be a good boy, or you know what Mama will do to you." She disconnected the call.

Deirdre glanced at Hansen to see his lips pressed together with consternation in the reflected light of passing cars. Was it about her or the threat?

"That how you play … your games?" he asked.

"I was only messing with him."

"You're mean."

"Sometimes. He's weak. I don't trust him."

"That stuff they say about you–guess it's true."

"Some of it."

"Well, it's none of my business."

She thought about reassuring him, but better he knew. She imagined suppressing her BDSM, or at least being Hansen's submissive. She'd make a good politician's wife and perhaps be the candidate herself someday. She'd be good at that too.

Her phone buzzed. The infotainment screen in the dashboard showed the call was from the US Senate sergeant at arms.

"Let it go," Hansen said.

"You sure? We could go to a hotel."

"What? Run because a legislative counsel in ODNI is saying someone is threatening my life?"

Why should he trust the FBI? Barstow's warning could well be more interference in his campaign.

"Want me to call Bobby?"

"No. I'll deal with it tomorrow." He sighed. "I don't know what's dirty tricks anymore. How do they know we're going to Redlands?"

"Our phones, I guess."

As they entered the cul-de-sac where the house was located, Deirdre noticed the old Honda parked in the darkened bend.

"You recognize that car?" Deirdre asked.

"No. But I'm not here that much."

"I don't like this. Let's go to a hotel."

"No. I'm not going to live my life in fear of strange cars. I told Tommy I'd take care of his dog."

The house was dark when they entered.

"Hello, Polly. Want to go out?" Hansen opened the sliding door, and the sheltie hurried into the backyard.

"Something smells in here," Deirdre said.

"Maybe something Polly dragged in," Hansen said. "Why aren't the Christmas lights on?" He looked into the dark living room.

Bastini stepped out of the hallway.

Deirdre reflexively assumed a fighting stance, balanced, ready.

Hansen's eyes narrowed. "Lauren," he said.

"The same," Bastini said, stepped into the kitchen, and motioned with her MAC aimed at them. The automatic weapon looked massively lethal, with an outsized magazine of bullets below a pistol. "Turn around, put your hands against the counter, spread your legs. Come on, you've seen the television shows. Do it like that."

Years of training in martial arts focused Deirdre on the threat. She controlled her heart rate and gauged what countermove to make and when.. A familiar contest for domination calmed her. Bastini's odor of someone who'd been on the street too long without a bath or change of clothes increased Dierdre's revulsion.

"What do you want?" Hansen's voice trembled.

Deirdre sensed his obvious fear would incite Bastini.

"Empty your pockets, coward. Put your purse on the counter, Deirdre Owens," Bastini said.

"What's your game?" Deirdre asked as if dealing in dominance and submission.

"Maybe what you did to Jake Gillium."

"Try to help him?" Deirdre asked.

"Yeah, you're going to help me now."

Like a deadly airport screening, they emptied their pockets and turned over their cellphones. Bastini patted them down to confirm they weren't armed.

"What do you want with us?" Hansen asked, turning his head.

"Don't move until I tell you," Bastini ordered.

Hansen's head turned back to a forward position.

"OK," Bastini said. "Here's what we're going to do. We're going on a trip. You'll drive. I'll sit in the back. If either of you try anything, I'll shoot one or the both of you. Call the dog."

"The dog?" Hansen asked.

"Call her," Bastini said.

Hansen walked slowly to the door and slid it open.

"Come on, girl."

The sheltie hurried inside, tail whipping back and forth, tongue out, eyes moving between the three of them.

---

Bastini stuffed Hansen's wallet and Deirdre's purse into the oversized white-fake-fur-topped pockets on the Santa frock.

She left their cellphones on. Let the feds think they were both in the house for as long as possible. If the IED she'd planted went off, they would think they'd been inside and waste more time looking for their remains.

She directed them through the kitchen to their rented SUV. "You drive," she instructed Deirdre. "You in the passenger seat." She motioned the pistol at Hansen.

"I've got to lower the windows," Deirdre said when they were all in.

"Leave them up."

"I can't stand the stench," Deirdre complained.

"Sorry, I didn't have time to bathe for the occasion."

"I'm going to vomit if I don't get some air," Deirdre said.

"That should make things smell better. Leave the windows up. Walk a mile in my shoes."

Bastini watched Deirdre reach over from the driver's seat and put her hand on Hansen's thigh, giving him an unflinching stare.

The woman had bigger balls than Hansen, but Bastini already knew Hansen was a sniveling coward. Maybe Deirdre loved him. Why should there be love all around Bastini while she was trapped in this body with her memories? She burned with the rage of the misplaced, the misbegotten, not sure when she was going to kill Hansen. Maybe offer him to a cartel. Imagine what a US senator would be worth.

"Where have you been, Lauren?" Hansen asked.

"Living it up."

"Can't say it's nice to see you under the circumstances," Hansen said.

"Can't help squirming, can you, coward? Keep your politician shit to yourself."

Deirdre lowered the driver's window.

"What did I tell you? Roll it up."

"What do you think I'm going to do? Jump out?" She reached over and turned on the heat and fan to full.

The woman was tough. Bastini thought about punishing her with a rap on the head with her gun barrel, but the air felt good. She tossed her cellphone out the window. Let the pigs figure that one out.

"I should shoot you both now."

"You won't," Deirdre said.

"How do you know?"

"You're not that kind of killer."

"How many people have I killed?"

Hansen's voice was thoughtful, as if trying to understand a problem. "How *could* you kill all those people, children? You burned down a day-care center."

"How many Iraqi or Afghan kids died in your war?"

"Wasn't my war," Hansen said.

Bastini's face reddened, and her hand tightened around the pistol handle. The *man* was always right, always privileged to rape the environment, to fill his pockets with loot, but never expecting or tolerating retribution. Bastini leaned forward, and Polly's head fell off her thigh. She pressed the barrel of the Berretta against the back of Hansen's head.

"Easy," Deirdre said.

Bastini's voice shook and came from deep in her gut. "You're weak and stupid, accomplices in this crime that's raping and pillaging the planet. Doom and destruction is all you offer."

As if trying to convince a reluctant voter, Deirdre said, "The senator has a 96 percent National Environmental Scorecard."

Bastini coughed a mocking snort. "He voted for the West Virginia pipeline."

"But he was able to trade that vote for an offshore wind farm in California," Deirdre argued.

Bastini scoffed. "I told you to keep your politician shit to yourself. Who are you to trade anything in nature?"

"You want to go back to the Stone Age?" Deirdre asked.

Hansen said assuredly, "Progress on environmental justice is slow, but it's coming."

Bastini huffed with a twisted sneer. "Retribution is coming. Mother Nature will have her way. I'm a small tool in the cure of the disease that is the human race."

Bastini leaned back, breathing rapidly through her nose. They'd crossed into the desert.

Streetlight domes on the dark horizon marked the water-wasting mansions and golf courses tended by Mexican immigrants. She wished she was in a plane loaded with hydrogen bombs. She wanted to kill this monster—not hurt or enrage it. What was her life worth? What had she done? She couldn't do this by herself. *Come, jihad. Hurry, my Muslim brothers, destroy Babylon before it sucks the last drop of righteous blood from the planet.*

She looked out into the dark horizon where Mexico lay. She had to stick to the plan and make it to the Middle East, where she could hide her body behind a black chador with her face veiled by a burqa. Inspire, offer guidance, and return to the fight when the time was right. She might be small and the enemy mighty, but she would never give up the struggle.

She hummed an Apache dirge in a hollow, warbling voice.

*Koo k lhadaa'dees'n l'a*
*Koo doojaa dabn go dla ldzaan l'a*
*Dooshdiits'adan n'shdeests'an l'a*
*Dooja da ija n jiisdl nl'a.*

If her previous behavior had not silenced her captives, her death chant ended any attempts by either to reason with her.

***

Two o'clock in the morning, East Coast time, Director of National Intelligence Uberhoff padded into the narrow kitchen of his two-bedroom DC apartment and started to reheat some stale coffee. His stomach burned with an acidic contraction, and he felt a fluttering in his chest that always made him think he was having a heart attack. His doctor had told him that it was from too much caffeine. He wondered if he could get a prescription for something. Maybe he should try some of the Adderall his kids took to concentrate.

Suddenly, his knees felt weak, and his head spun. He leaned against the counter and waited for the spell to pass. For the hundredth time, he thought of the impossibility of his job. People in business had no idea what pressure was.

Look at the havoc a scrawny crisp of an old American lady with a gripe was causing. And this was just the beginning, an early stage of development, like the computer industry in the eighties. Look how fast that had morphed–products and technologies chasing each other out of the market. Terrorists today were adapting and becoming more sophisticated. The raw materials for mass destruction were everywhere–radioactive and chemical waste–and factories, businesses, and population centers were open and accessible targets for their bombs. Despite this cornucopia of deadly tools, the country wanted—demanded—freedom. He pitied and could not imagine what his successors would face.

Uberhoff yawned, took his coffee from the microwave, and returned to the living room. His phone rang, patched through from the ODNI operations center.

A search warrant had been issued based on probable cause of felony breaking and entering into the senator's official residence. A stingray, a portable cellphone tower, had revealed two active cellphones belonging to Hansen and Deirdre Owens inside the home. Efforts to reach both had gone unanswered. A car parked in front of the house with a stolen license plate had been matched with a surveillance video from a bus station near the Mission Inn. FBI digital forensics reported that the phone that had made the call to Blum's cellphone had been traced to a stationary spot in the desert.

Thermal sensors had detected no body signatures in the house; possibly a stove had been left on. AFT explosive-sniffing dogs had alerted them to explosives, and the neighbors had been advised to evacuate or shelter in place away from windows.

An alert had been issued for a car rented by Deirdre Owens.

Uberhoff had to give the final permission to enter the home of a US senator.

The operation was based on Blum. Well, he'd been right about the Mission Inn. The old agent was like a bloodhound on the scent. But what if he was wrong and they were about to burst into the home of a US senator who could well be shacking up with a woman, not his wife? Wouldn't that make a tantalizing story? Hansen would have firsthand proof of the government's overreach, and have evidence to limit the tools they needed–were using this minute–to peer inside his home.

They might find the senator, but what about Bastini? Even with all their surveillance resources, with the number of agents tracking her,

her name and scarred face as publicized as Osama bin Laden—she'd reportedly driven across the continent to pop up in a Santa costume at the Mission Inn.

She was more dangerous and more destructive than any foreign terrorist. She was a pair of scissors cutting through the fabric of trust that held a civil community together, allowing democracy to exist. She epitomized the essential threat of terrorism–that a terrorist could be anyone–a grandmother or a white American radical from West Virginia–that a single person could attack, destroy, and move about freely in a free society. The terrible truth of modern terrorism is that anyone and everyone could be the enemy. And when everyone is the enemy, there can be no trust, and without trust, there can be no freedom, and without freedom, there can be no democracy.

The whole show was ready to go. Full agency response initiated. A hostage rescue team was at the address.

They'd gone too far not to enter the house. "Ahem. Proceed," Uberhoff said.

He hung up and hunched over his knees, exhausted. This event might end soon with disaster or drag on into a search for a United States senator and a deranged seventy-three-year-old eco-terrorist. He was tempted to go back to sleep but was afraid he wouldn't be able to wake up for the next update.

## FIFTEEN

## BOMBING RANGE

Deirdre pulled into a gas station outside of Yuma off Interstate 8. Bastini trained her pistol on her. "I'll be watching you. Keep your face to the car. If I see you try anything, I'll shoot you both."

Deirdre nodded gravely and opened the passenger door. The dog Polly whined and tried to get out with her.

"She, shh." Bastini tried to calm her.

"She has to go," Hansen said.

Bastini held the sheltie around her neck. "Close the door. She'll be all right."

"I have to go too," Deirdre said.

"Pee in your pants if you have to," Bastini said.

"Join the club," Deirdre said.

"Life's rough," Bastini said. "We'll stop when we get off the road. Pump the damn gas and get back in the car."

Deirdre climbed from the car. She shivered from the combination of nerves and the December desert chill. The barrel of Bastini's pistol was aimed at her through the window.

There must be surveillance cameras somewhere. *Please be watching, somebody. This is not normal.*

Beyond the gas station's pole lights was dark, open, and wild desert.

She might escape and get help, but as soon as she turned to run, Bastini would fire. Bastini had nothing to lose and was ready to die. And what about Hansen? Even if Deirdre evaded the bullets, Hansen could be killed. Who was to say that they weren't already as good as dead? The difference was Bastini choosing the time and place.

She felt a familiar thrill and was surprised to sense she was enjoying real bondage, not sexual or consensual submission, no misguided love or games, domination by might, pure expression of power and control. She would play the submissive until the time was right for her to dominate. Ugly attraction was part of the game.

Face tense with pressed lips and narrowed eyes, Deirdre climbed back into the driver's seat.

Bastini handed Hansen a piece of paper. "Follow these directions. Don't get back on the freeway."

Deirdre started to drive. Bastini returned to an upright position. They followed the road south. The houses marked by outside lights were spaced farther apart, resting on arid lots of cacti and gravel.

"I can't read it, it's too dark," Hansen said.

Bastini cursed and crouched down on the floor again. "Turn on the overhead light."

The single light shone down from the car ceiling.

"We're looking for a canal. There it is." He pointed to an embankment.

"Turn off the light," Bastini ordered.

In the darkness, Hansen directed Deirdre to a dirt road beside the canal. "There's a bridge, cross here," he said.

Deirdre slowly guided the SUV onto a narrow wooden bridge and a dirt road until they came to a break in the wire and wood-pole fencing.

"I'm going to turn the light on again, just for a minute," Hansen said, quickly reading the directions. "We're looking for a sign for the Circle Bar Ten Ranch," he said, turning off the lights.

Deirdre noted Hansen's submission, maybe the same Stockholm syndrome that had driven Patty Hearst to rob a bank.

The car rocked as it passed over the rutted road. "There it is," Hansen said.

Deirdre slowed the car to a crawl.

"There's a lock on the gate," Hansen said.

Bastini peered out the side window. The light of a quarter moon showed a barbwire fence and undulating desert hills. "Go down three poles," she said. "Stop here. Get out of the car. Both of you."

Deirdre and Hansen climbed from the car.

"Stay where I can see you," Bastini said to Hansen. "Girls over here." She led Deirdre to where they were facing each other, with Bastini watching Hansen.

Deirdre pulled down her panties and squatted.

From that position, face-to-face with Bastini, she could see the age and hardship in the scars and lined skin. "You into pain?" she asked.

The question was so unexpected that it broke through Bastini's hard front. She blinked and focused on Deirdre from a similar squat. "What?"

"This is torture. I thought you might enjoy it, you know, giving pain."

Bastini pulled up her pants. "I've had enough pain in my life."

"So have I," Deirdre said.

Bastini studied her. "What are you, his whore?"

"Sometimes," Deirdre said.

For the first time, she felt a connection. Bastini barely smiled.

Polly stared out into the darkness with her ears pricked and wiped her tongue over her snout, smelling the strange scents and listening to the rhythmic chirping of insects and the rustle of mesquite trees. A coyote howled in the dark.

Hansen started back to the car.

"Stay where I can see you," Bastini ordered.

The senator stepped away from the car and whispered to Deirdre. "It's going to be OK."

"No talking!" Bastini ordered.

Deirdre saw Hansen tense as if ready to jump Bastini. She calmed him with a hand on his arm.

Bastini must have sensed or anticipated Hansen's attempt. The gun pistol shook in her hand.

Deirdre kept her hand on Hansen's upper arm.

Bastini stepped slowly toward them. "How many people have I killed? How many?" she seethed and aimed the pistol between Hansen's eyes.

"Stop." Deirdre's tone was commanding, not pleading. "You never killed a lover."

Bastini's eyes slid to her. "How do you know that?"

"The news. You two are star-crossed lovers in some people's eyes."

Bastini's posture relaxed slightly. For a moment, she and Hansen stared at each other as if remembering when she'd taken an innocent's virginity at Cal. "Yeah, doomed to a tragic ending," she said.

Deirdre had sensed the game in Bastini—dominate or be dominated. Bastini was a submissive. Deirdre wasn't afraid anymore. Bastini wouldn't kill them. She didn't kill face-to-face.

Bastini motioned with the gun toward Deirdre. "Who do you think is in charge here?"

"You are, dear," Deirdre said.

Bastini's flicker of a grin neared a smile. "Damn, you're crazier than I am."

Deirdre didn't respond with humor. "What next?" she asked as if to an employee.

"The third section down from the gate, lift the pole."

Deirdre led Hansen up the slight embankment.

"I've got this," Deirdre whispered.

"She's going to kill us anyway," Hansen said.

"No talking!"

The pole lifted easily out of the ground. "Pull it aside," Bastini ordered.

They drove through, and Hansen closed the hidden passage behind them.

"Turn off your lights," Bastini instructed and activated a preprogrammed nautical GPS unit she'd taken from the duffle bag.

A woman's voice said, "You are twenty degrees off course to the port."

"Turn on the four-wheel drive and head right some," Bastini said.

Deirdre searched for a way to engage all four wheels. "I don't see how," she said.

"You are ten degrees off course to the starboard," the unit said.

"Back the other way," Bastini said. "What about you?" She tapped Hansen on the shoulder. "You know?"

"Want me to stop and look?" Deirdre asked.

"Keep driving."

Deirdre's eyes adjusted to the dark, and she could see the barren nightscape through which they were slowly passing along a deserted, rutted road. Did Bastini intend to drive cross-country into Mexico? What was this place? To ask would be to show weakness. Never show fear.

They moved cross-country down into a rain wash and up to a low pass through a pair of hills. Deirdre studied lights on the other side of a dry wash and figured they marked the house of the owner of the land, who had either been paid or threatened into not asking questions.

In the distance was a low rumbling sound that grew louder as they drove into the night. The thumping was shaking the car.

They came to another fence. A sign read:

*DANGER*
*USAF GUNNERY RANGE*
*DO NOT ENTER*
*PELIGRO*
*NO ENTRAR*

Again, they were able to lift out a post and pull back a section to pass.

After fifteen minutes of following the same direction, they came to the top of a rise where a vast stretch marked by gullies and dry riverbeds was visible in the faint moonlight. The ground vibrated, and jets roared overhead. In the distance, explosions flared, followed by reports–some deeper *thump-thumps*, others low rumblings and shockwaves that rolled over the car, pressing against her eardrums.

"We can't go down there," Hansen said.

"Drive, damn it," Bastini pressed the pistol barrel against Deirdre's head.

"Put the gun down!" Deirdre ordered and tried to steer a course that wouldn't tip the SUV over.

They dropped down into a low plain and drove toward the explosions. To the right, lights were moving toward them.

"Stop," Bastini ordered. "Pull under that tree."

The sound of helicopters competed with the reports of bombs and missiles. Two sets of lights circled over where they were heading. The dog whined and trembled.

Lights flashed on from a car a quarter of a mile ahead of them. Laser sighting beams and searchlights painted the pickup racing up the barranca. As the truck passed fifty yards from them, Deirdre could see terrified illegal immigrant faces clinging for their lives as the truck rocked and bounced violently over the undulating surface for a dubious chance to escape.

"Poor bastards," Bastini muttered as the nefarious caravan passed, returning the desert to its relative silence. "Drive," she said.

The GPS guided them south across a bajada, past gullies and washes toward the dark slope of mountains. Night swallowed the visible distance. Deirdre saw what looked like old shipping containers, some blown up and twisted into metal strips stacked atop one another to form targets. She quickly drove through the target zone, past a tank with a barrel bent at a right angle to the turret.

The GPS said, "You're ten degrees off course to the starboard."

They passed through a field of craters with white parachutes looking like strange planting. Deirdre swerved to avoid a bomb pit, and they slid down an embankment. The rear of the SUV fishtailed and became stuck in the sand.

The engine whined, and the wheels dug in deeper. Deirdre stopped trying to power out of the rut.

"Put it in four-wheel drive," Bastini said.

"Tell me how," Hansen said.

"Look in the glove compartment for the manual," Bastini said.

Hansen found the book and turned on the overhead light. With his reading glasses, he looked like the professor he'd been.

"It's constant four-wheel drive," he reported. "We have to get out. Put something under the wheels or dig out."

A whistling and a series of explosions were followed by the thunder-like report of jets breaking the sound barrier. The SUV was lifted and thrown around so violently it felt like it would tip over—a spiderweb of cracks traced across the windshield. The violent motion knocked them free, and they were moving again, swaying as they passed over the pocked earth.

"You're fifteen degrees off course to the port. You're thirty degrees . . ." Deirdre ignored the GPS as they raced through the killing field.

Then the desert was still.

"It's stopped," Bastini said. "Slow down."

"You are eighty degrees off course to the port."

"Turn that way." Bastini pointed into the darkness.

The car began to shudder in a manner distinct from the violent rocking. "We have a flat," Deirdre said.

"Keep driving," Bastini ordered, but it soon became apparent the car could only lumber forward at a few miles per hour, almost as if the wheel was falling over itself. The SUV shuddered to a stop.

"We're stuck again," Deirdre said.

"Then get it unstuck," Bastini said.

"We're going to have to change the tire," Hansen said.

"Do it."

Bastini climbed out of the car, holding her terrifying weapon on them.

Stars were resplendent in the dark scape lit only by the fractional moon. Deirdre thought if she was to die here, she'd be closer to heaven. She wasn't going to die, not here, shot or blown up. Hers was another destiny. She didn't know when or how she was going to die, but it wasn't going to be here. She waited for her chance to assert control.

Bastini watched Hansen open the rear hatchback to retrieve the jack and tire iron. Polly clamored out and frolicked excitedly between them.

Bastini reached in the back seat for the dog leash. For an instant, her back was turned. Deirdre thought about trying to use her kickboxing to overpower the woman but sparring in a gym was not trying to land a punch or kick on someone with a gun on uncertain ground.

Hansen bent over, trying to place the base of the jack to lift the car. He found some wood in a sand wash to stabilize the jack in the loose sand.

Polly growled, pulled on the leash, and barked, her back arched, teeth bared, toward a creosote bush. The hoot of a great horned owl was answered by the trill of another night bird.

Bastini aimed the rifle. Polly barked, looked over her shoulder at them, and barked again into the darkness.

Whoever was out there was not coming into view. Deirdre figured it was a coyote or illegals. Border patrol or MPs would have heard the dog and come to investigate.

Bastini's eyes darted between Deirdre and the perimeter. Suddenly, the dark sky was patterned by the slowly descending lights of parachute flares. Over the next rise, the scream of a low-flying jet was followed by a bright flash and explosion.

Deirdre fell to a crouch and instinctively cowered. The reverberation passed them with a chemical scent of explosives and desert dust.

Moaning and crying came from less than fifty yards away.

"Somebody's hurt," Hansen said.

Bastini snorted. "Beautiful karma if you were to be blown up by the bombs you voted for. But I don't want to go with you. Get that tire changed."

The sound of shuffling feet and movement caused Bastini to aim into the dark.

A group approached cautiously. Three men, two teenage boys, and three women came into view. A woman with a broad face and the high cheekbones of an indigenous native was holding a baby.

Deirdre could see their fear in the moonlight, how they leaned as if to run, then looked back at them, more afraid of what was out there than Bastini and her rifle.

"*¿Estás herido?*" Hansen asked. "*¿Qué pasó?*"

An older woman stepped forward, speaking for the group. She looked at Hansen, but her eyes often went to Bastini and the gun. "*Él nos estaba llevando a través. Dijo que conocía el camino. Algo cayó, una bomba creo.*"

The moaning had stopped.

"Tire changed? You're good for something. Get back in the car," Bastini said.

"What about them?" Hansen asked.

Bastini leveled the barrel at his chest. "You can stay with them if you want."

He stood straighter, looking her in the eye.

"*Cuidate,*" Hansen said to the woman. "*Probablemente deberías volver, probar de otra manera.*"

The immigrants stared at them as if they were their last hope, a devil's bargain. Parachute flares lit up the sky as they slowly descended.

Deirdre took several deep breaths. The time for action was nearing. The raucous howl of coyotes indicated the shared joy of a kill or a death in the pack.

The shadow of an owl swooped overhead, distracting Bastini long enough for Deirdre to jab, cross, and round-kick the side of Bastini's chest. The kick felt good, like a solid punch on the bag.

The quick combination spun Bastini toward Hansen, who swung the tire iron at her.

The blow glanced off Bastini's scalp and came down on her shoulder. She cried out and tried to raise the rifle.

*Just like the bag,* Deirdre told herself as she cross-punched and kicked Bastini in the chest.

Bastini fell backward.

Deirdre picked up the fallen rifle, though she'd never held, much less shot, one. Her exaltation was unlike anything she'd ever felt.

Bastini tried to get up.

"Slowly," Deirdre said.

"You're not going to shoot me," Bastini said.

"I can sure give you another kick. Take the bag from her," she said to Hansen.

"Careful," Bastini said as Hansen lifted the bag over a shoulder that hung at an unnatural angle. "God, it hurts."

"Get in the car. We have to get out of here," Hansen said. "They could start again any minute. *Súbase al auto,*" he said to the illegals.

Bastini turned and ran awkwardly with one hand holding the arm of her broken shoulder. Deirdre watched her disappear into the darkness. She looked at Hansen and knew neither would attempt to follow her.

As the illegals packed themselves into the back of the SUV, a bright flash and shock wave rolled over them from the direction where Bastini had run.

Deirdre flinched and looked at Hansen, who pressed his lips together and sighed, knowing that, most likely, Bastini had stepped on an antipersonnel mine.

Deirdre held the GPS in the passenger seat, trying to figure out how to program their way back through the metal shards, explosives, and sand pits.

＊＊＊

Blum was in the second team that entered the house looking for evidence that Bastini had kidnapped Allan Hansen and Deirdre Owens. He wore an outer tactical vest to protect his chest, and a high-density polyethylene helmet with *FBI* stenciled on the front.

The dogs had found the IED attached to the Christmas tree, a very powerful bomb that would have leveled Hansen's and several neighbors' houses.

His phone rang. Barstow was in the operations center. A surveillance video outside of Yuma had matched the SUV with Deirdre Owens's rental.

"She's on the move. Has the senator," Blum said.

"And Deirdre," Barstow said with a slip of personal concern.

Blum turned to leave for Yuma.

Shots came from the kitchen.

Blum flinched and turned.

A pressure cooker with bullets triggered explosives. Wooden splinters from the cabinet where Bastini had placed the bomb entered Blum's right eye. He was dead by the time the force of the explosion threw him into the dining room, and the roof collapsed over him.

<hr>

At 10:30 a.m., Uberhoff was in the Oval Office giving the president his daily security briefing. The early winter sunlight slanted in from expansive windows leading to the Rose Garden. It caused his vision to blur with floaters passing across his retina. The DNI had only slept for a few hours the previous night. Whatever refreshment he'd derived from the shower he'd taken before rushing to the White House quickly faded. The rule was that he and the president were not to be interrupted except for emergencies, so when the phone rang on the president's desk, Uberhoff knew it was important.

"Good." The president smiled and placed the receiver back in its cradle. "They've found Hansen. Let's take it in the Situation Room."

Uberhoff never got tired of being around the president. No matter what he thought of the man, the office and the White House concealed flaws and magnified his power and leadership.

The permanent National Security Council staff made the liaisons from the Office of the Director of National Intelligence redundant. The NSC staff was a well-coordinated team with access to federal agencies when needed to serve the president. His ODNI team was a loose amalgamation of agencies, but they'd shown their stuff on the Bastini matter.

"What do we have?" the president asked, sitting at the head of the table.

A woman whose firm, tinted hair framed a long narrow face gave the initial briefing. "A maritime distress signal was picked up from the Goldwater bombing range."

A red dot on an electronic map on the wall marked the location near the Mexican border where the call had originated. The area around the dot was shaded in blue and marked as an air force bombing range.

"The senator and his party were found by an Air Force search and rescue team standing by at the request of the director of national intelligence. The party includes a campaign aide, Deirdre Owens, and a party of illegal immigrants."

"More illegals." The president frowned. "Any sign of Bastini?" he asked.

"No, sir. The senator believes she was killed by some of the unexploded ordnance in the range. We are searching for her remains."

"What about that FBI agent that was killed?"

"His name was George Blum, sir," the aide said.

"Yes, George Blum. I want to call his family, give him a posthumous award. He was a real hero."

Uberhoff knew the president couldn't care less about Blum's family. He would most likely use the call to talk about himself. "Ahem. Think Senator Hansen will be more supportive of our domestic intelligence-gathering needs?" Uberhoff asked.

"Doubt it," said the president. "He'll probably find some way to blame me for the whole escapade. But he's going to be hard to beat. Voters love a good story."

# SIXTEEN

## CODA: PAIN

Three years after she'd escaped from Bastini, Deirdre walked up the stairs into the Federal-style brick town house she now shared with Hansen.

The president had been right. Hansen won his reelection by a narrow margin. Rather than run from the story, they were able to embrace the heroics of Allan Hansen. His claim of fighting terrorism rang truer than promises. What could the gun lobby say against a politician who had disarmed a terrorist holding a MAC-10 on him? Voters were also understanding of him leaving his wife to live with the woman who had battled at his side in desert combat.

Deirdre picked up a pile of mail off a marble-top baluster table and carried it into the office where Hansen was working his way through a list of likely contributors.

On the speakerphone, Deirdre heard a woman lecture. "I saw the movie about you. You're very brave."

"I did what I had to do," Hansen said wearily.

"And they still haven't found that woman's body? Do you think she survived?"

Hansen looked at Deirdre. "We don't know."

"All right, put me down for two thousand dollars."

"How about twenty-five hundred? California is a very expensive place to run a statewide campaign."

"All right, put me down for twenty-five hundred."

"Thanks very much, Ethene."

Deirdre flipped through the mail, the usual bills, advertisements, and invitations to fundraisers. She came to a thin blue envelope marked with *Par Avion*. The letter was addressed to her in neat handwriting and had no return address. The stamp was in Arabic. She couldn't tell from what country.

A warning told her to drop it.

"We better get out of here."

"Why?" Hansen asked.

"There's something about this letter I don't like. It was delivered here, so I don't think it's been inspected."

Hansen looked at the letter. "Ricin?"

"Or worse."

He frowned and stood up to leave. "I've learned to listen to you. Can't be too careful."

"That's a good boy."

---

Obeying her was good for him in many ways.

Inside had been white powder identified by the US Capitol Police as ricin, a highly toxic product of castor oil seeds.

Also, inside was a picture of a woman in a burqa with an inscription on the back in the same neat cursive as the address: *You into pain?*

# CAST OF CHARACTERS

**Alex Uberhoff**: Director of the Office of National Intelligence (ODNI), the agency tasked with coordinating the 18 intelligence agencies of the federal government.

**Ali Shaifqueur**: Pakistani arms smuggler, cousin of **Shaquat Hailakandi.**

**Allan Hansen** (aka **Allan Ali Hansen**): US Senator and senate candidate from California.

**Ameri Battlestone**: landlord of **Deirdre Owens** and civil rights lawyer concerned about the rise of rightwing totalitarianism in the United States.

**Angela Parkston**: Stanford professor of **Ameri Battlestone** who lectured on Oakland 4.

**Annie Metcalf**: media consultant tasked with preparing **Deirdre Owens** for going on a talk show to defend **Allan Hansen.**

**Anthony Belligoni**: Assistant US Attorney asked by federal judge **June Wallace** to investigate the release of the COPCOM files concerning **Senator Allan Hansen.**

**Barbara Stein**: movie actress whose Malibu home is bugged by FBI to entrap **Senator Allan Hansen.**

**Bobby Sutton**: **Allan Hansen** senate campaign security.

**Brooke**: TV reporter reporting on nuclear attack.

**Cliffy**: undercover alias of FBI Agent **George Blum** to entrap the Oakland 4.

**Corinth**: editor Sacramento BEE newspaper.

**Cork Johnson**: Los Angeles Police Department (LAPD) detective collected evidence that implicated **Allan Hansen.**

**Craig Masterson**: Cove Point Liquid Natural Gas (LNG) facility worker.

**Deirdre Owens**: campaign manager for **Senator Allan Hansen.**

**Dennis Dalleck**: Assistant US Attorney in Los Angeles, a political hack implementing White House push to implicate **Senator Hansen** in the Oakland 4 terrorist group.

**Ethene**: campaign contributor.

**Franny:** wife **George Blum**.

**George Blum** (aka Cliffy): senior FBI agent assigned as investigator in the office of Assistant US Attorney **Dennis Dalleck.** Later, assigned to the Office of the Director of National Intelligence to capture or kill **Lauren Bastini.**

**Greg Thompson**: Office of Director of National Intelligence (ODNI) lawyer.

**Jack Mastanza**: television reporter.

**Jacob Gillium**: college freshman roommate of **Senator Allan Hansen** at UC Berkeley, a convicted member of Oakland 4, college roommate of **Allan Hansen.**

**James Heikes**: Director of FBI.

**Jefferies:** Supreme Court Justice.

**Jerry Sabah**: FBI Assistant Director.

**Jim Branson**: Director of Domestic Security Association (DSA), a public interest organization hired by FBI to put pressure on **Lauren Bastini**.

**Jimmy Tolver**: leader of Oakland 4 killed while attempting to bomb research facility.

**Joe Upton**: chief of staff **Senator Allan Hansen**.

**June Wallace** (aka Lady June Bug): federal judge asked by **Ameri Battlestone** to investigate the release of evidence implicating **Senator Hansen** in the death of **Jake Gillium**.

**Hillary Morgenstern**: US Attorney, political appointee trying to kill the investigation into the release of the **Hansen** evidence.

**Kahlid Shaifqueur**: Pakistani arms dealer.

**Krisky**: FBI assistant director.

**Larry Gerse**: LAPD detective.

**Larry Grogan**: Editor States Affairs Bureau Sacramento Bee newspaper.

**Lauren Bastini** (the Gray Anarchist)**:** convicted Oakland 4 conspirator, thought to have evidence implicating **Senator Hansen** in plot to firebomb the Monsanto research facility in Berkeley when a roommate of **Jacob Gillium.**

**Lawrence Yushima**: Assistant US attorney, pressured **Allen Hansen** to testify against **Jacob Gillium** about attempted fire-bombing of Monsanto research facility.

**Lyle Cinquist**: security Mission Inn Riverside.

**Lyons**: US Senate Majority Leader.

**Mary Regina**: television personality.

**Matthew Sorensen**: CIA deputy director.

**Mavis:** TV studio makeup artist.

**Michael Flemings**: television producer.

**Michelle Chang**: LAPD evidence technician.

**Mike Tahaji**: National Reconnaissance Office official assigned to Office of the Director of National Intelligence (ONDI).

**Milo Tooley**: White House National Security Advisor.

**Missy Compton**: Department of Energy Nuclear staffer assigned to Office of the Director of National Intelligence (ODNI).

**Mizz G/Gertrude Gillium**: mother of **Jacob Gillium**, store owner.

**Morgan Lancaster**: White House aide, leaker of the COPCOM file.

**Papa Dave**: grandfather of **Lauren Bastini**.

**Paul Barstow**: lawyer Office Director of National Intelligence (ODNI), consensual bondage (BDSM) partner to **Deirdre Owens**.

**Pedro Miscalente**: military aide Director of National Intelligence (ONDI) **Alex Uberhoff.**

**Peta Whiltlison**: staff Domestic Security Association.

**Polly** (a dog).

**Captain Randal**: US Coast Guard assigned to Office of the Director of National Intelligence (ONDI).

**Raymond Patterson**: U.S. Attorney General.

**Reggie Delatore**: security director Cover Point LNG facility.

**Rick Rage**: right-wing radio host.

**Roger Hartman**: television personality.

**Shaquat Hailakandi**: Pakistani refuge hiding with his family in the basement of **Lauren Bastini**.

**Tommy**: brother Senator Allen Hansen.

**Willard Mastroni**: FBI agent.

**Willis Gradisky**: editor Poliscope, a political blog and website that first publishes evidence of **Senator Hansen** involvement in a possible crime

**JEFFREY MARCUS OSHINS** worked on the national security staff of the US Congress for eleven years with a focus on military sealift. He is the founder of NatPrep (www.natprep.com) providing homeland security consulting to domestic and foreign clients. He worked in the port of Skikda, Algeria a year after an explosion in the LNG facility there had flattened much of the port and city. The Gray Anarchist is his sixth published book (www.jmobooks.com). Jeffrey Marcus Oshins was a candidate for Congress from the Central Coast of California in 2016. He has also worked on the campaign staff of three presidential campaigns.

www.ingramcontent.com/pod-product-compliance
Lightning Source LLC
Chambersburg PA
CBHW031110260626
47172CB00001B/293